I0713416

Cover design by **Holly Symons**
Black Edition

For More, Please Visit
HollySymons.com.au

"By the balls of Odin, she's mine."

I am
Polyonymous
And every night I live, dream walking

HOLLY SYMONS

Chapter One – The Queen of Many Names

The sea struck against the longships like drums of war. Mist clung to the horizon, heavy as fate,
and gulls wheeled overhead, crying warnings that no warrior listened to.

Polyonymous stood at the prow, her hair a pale river, lashes wet with salt.
The men called her queen, and indeed she was, yet in her veins burned something older than crowns or iron.
Her people whispered that she carried a thousand names, each belonging to a different self.
At her back stood Ragnar. Broad as the shields that bore his crest, wrapped in furs that smelled of blood and fire.
His hand rested on her hip, firm, claiming, but

not cruel. He was a man who ruled by strength, not fear yet the storm in his eyes revealed he was not blind to her distance.

"Another raid won," he murmured, his beard brushing her ear.
"The gods favour us. Tonight, we drink. Tomorrow, we take what is ours."

Polyonymous leaned into him, letting his warmth steady her.
To the men, they looked unbreakable, the golden pair of a Norse saga.

But beneath her ribs, her heartbeat in uneven rhythm, tugged by threads that stretched far beyond fjords and firelit halls.
When she looked at the horizon, she saw not mist but doors.
And she knew that when the night fell, one would open for her again.

Chapter Two – The Queen and the Hearthfire

The mead hall roared with victory. Shields clashed, songs rose, and fire licked the rafters in golden tongues.

Ragnar drank deep, laughter booming, his hand gripping Polyonymous's thigh as though to anchor her here, in this mortal joy.

Yet she felt the distance, like a veil of glass. The mead was sweet but thin, the voices a chorus half-faded.

She smiled when spoken to, touched Ragnar's cheek when he kissed her, but her eyes drifted always to the shadows at the edge of the hall, where dream already pressed against waking.

Later, when the revelry dimmed and the warriors stumbled to their beds, Ragnar carried her to their chamber.

His body was a furnace, his love fierce. He whispered her name as though it were his prayer, his anchor to the world.
And for a moment, she let herself believe she belonged wholly here, in this bed, in this skin.

But when his breath slowed beside her, when silence coiled around the longhouse, she felt the pull.

Her pulse quickened. Her breath hitched. The fire's glow blurred, and the weight of Ragnar's arm across her waist grew heavy as stone.

The world tilted.

And Polyonymous, the queen with a thousand names, slipped into the dark.

Interlude 1 – The Stone-Kissed King

The mountains bled fire where the sky split open.

Polyonymous drifted into the dream and found herself armoured, her braid heavy down her back, her breath hot against the cold wind. The cliffs rose jagged around her, trembling with each heartbeat of the land itself.

He emerged from the stone.

A giant of horn and granite, his flesh ridged like the mountain face, his eyes smouldering amber.

The people of this realm whispered his name only in fear Karnath, the Stone-Kissed King. They called him cursed, doomed to rule alone, his heart buried under the weight of the earth itself.

But when he looked at her, the curse trembled.

Polyonymous did not flinch as he loomed over
her, nor when the ground quaked with his
steps.
Her hand rose, unbidden, brushing the hard
plane of his chest.
It was like touching molten stone heat trapped
beneath centuries of armour.

"You should fear me," he growled, voice like
grinding rock.

"And yet," she whispered, "I do not."

His horns framed her face as he bent low, his
massive form closing her in.
The world around them roared with fire and
storm, yet in the stillness between their
mouths, there was only breath, only want, only
the sharp ache of being seen.

When her lips met his, it was as if the
mountain cracked.

The kiss was not gentle it was seismic,
shattering, pulling her into a depth that had no
end.

He clutched her as though he could keep her,
stone fingers trembling against her softness.

But already the dream unravelled.
Already the mountain began to collapse into
smoke and silence.

His roar followed her as she was torn away,
ripped back to the furs of her Norse bed.

And as she gasped awake, she felt the taste of
stone still burning on her lips.

Chapter Three – Dreki, the Flame of Mischief

Flashback:

The mountains had been quiet that morning, the mist low and silver on the fjords. Ragnar had walked alone, his axe strapped across his back, seeking silence after too many nights of blood and song.

That was when he heard it a whimper, soft as wind through reeds.

He found the nest among the rocks: the mother dragon lay still, her scales dulled to stone, her massive body fallen in final slumber. But beside her, pressed against her unmoving flank, was a tiny creature scales ebony and red, eyes wide with terror and hunger.

The little dragon hissed weakly, wings too small to spread, trembling as Ragnar crouched near.

Slowly, Ragnar laid down his weapon and pulled dried meat from his pouch. He tore it into pieces, holding them out. The dragon sniffed, blinked, then, with a hungry squeak, devoured the food. When it finished, it butted its head into Ragnar's hand, demanding more.

A laugh rumbled from his chest. "So fierce, and yet so small."

He lifted the creature gently, the tiny claws clinging to his tunic, the warm scales pressed to his neck. The dragon gave a sigh, eyes closing as it burrowed into Ragnar's shoulder.

"You have seen enough battles for one so small," he whispered. "Come home with me, little one. I shall call you Dreki."

Present Day:

Polyonymous woke with a start not from Ragnar's warmth at her side, but from the hot gust of breath against her cheek. She opened her eyes to find herself staring into two enormous firey orbs.

"By the gods!" she gasped, recoiling.

The eyes blinked. Then Dreki, no longer the trembling hatchling but now the size of a pony, wagged his tail like a golden retriever. A stream of drool slipped from his jaw and splattered onto the sheets.

"Ewww, you naughty little beast!" Polyonymous scolded, wiping her arm.

"Where is your master, hmm?"

With a chirping growl, Dreki bounced after her as she left the chamber. His claws clicked on the wooden floor, wings flapping clumsily, knocking a shield from the wall as he bounded along.

In the longhouse's hearth-hall, she found Ragnar bare-chested, bare-legged, and singing a Viking song off-key as he turned a pan over the fire. He spun around, grinning, his hair loose, beard wild, and thrust a slice of fruit between her lips before she could protest.

"Breakfast for my queen," he said, kissing her fiercely.

She chewed, swallowed, then glared down at him. "And where are your pants? How is a king ready for battle without armour for his legs?"

Ragnar pulled her close, his lips trailing down her neck. "The only battle I fight this morning is feeding and loving my wife."

Behind them, Dreki eyed the table. His long tongue darted out and snatched an entire smoked fish, bones and all.

"Dreki, no" Polyonymous began.

The dragon hiccupped. Then belched.

A burst of flame shot across the hall and caught Ragnar squarely on the backside.

"AAAAHHHH!" he roared, leaping into the air, clutching his scorched rear. "By Odin's hairy balls!"

Polyonymous doubled over in laughter as
Ragnar danced in circles, fanning his
smouldering furs. "Polyonymous, you were
right! No warrior should go to battle bare
arsed especially when the enemy sleeps under
his own roof!"

Dreki blinked innocently, then gave another
hiccup, smoke curling from his nostrils.

Ragnar scowled, rubbing his burned rump.
"Well. At least the beast has singed away my
bum hair. That's one less chore for you, wife."

He stormed off to find pants, muttering curses.

Polyonymous knelt, stroking Dreki's scaly
snout. "You definitely keep him on his toes,"
she whispered with a giggle.

The dragon purred, pressing his head against her hand, as if to agree.

Chapter Four – The Market of Ash and Stone

The kingdom breathed with life that morning. Stalls spilled over with pelts and antlers, the clang of iron ringing out where smiths hammered new blades, the air sweet with honey-wine and roasting boar. Ragnar's hand was heavy and warm around hers as he guided her through the market, his blue cloak sweeping the dirt like a king who forgot to walk like one.

"Look at you," Polyonymous teased, tugging on his cloak. "Striding like a god who misplaced his throne."

Ragnar grinned, leaning close enough to brush her temple with his beard. "My throne is wherever you stand, wife."

"Careful," she said, laughing as she slipped a fur cap onto his head, the earflaps dangling ridiculously. "The people may mistake you for a bear."

"And what of it? Better a bear than a lovesick pup." He caught her wrist, kissed her knuckles, then slipped the cap onto her head instead. "There. Now we're both ridiculous."

They wove deeper into the stalls, pausing to trade coin for a gleaming pauldron chased in silver, for furs soft as snowfall. Children darted around them, their laughter bright against the morning sun. For a moment, the world felt untouched by war.

Until the ground trembled.

A low thunder rolled beneath their feet, making jars rattle and shields crash from their hooks. Merchants screamed. Ragnar drew her behind him, his hand flying to the axe at his back.

From the edge of the market, the cobblestones cracked. Stone split like brittle ice, and a figure rose from the earth itself horned, colossal, eyes burning amber.

Polyonymous's heart clenched. She knew him.

Karnath. The Stone-Kissed King.

He roared, the sound like boulders grinding together, and swung a fist that sent stalls splintering. Warriors rushed forward, blades flashing, but he swept them aside as though swatting flies.

"Stay back!" Ragnar barked, lunging at the giant's leg with his axe. Sparks burst where steel bit stone.

Polyonymous tried to run to him, but Karnath's hand closed around her, crushing the air from her lungs as he lifted her high. She gasped, clawing at his grip.

Then his forehead pressed to hers.

The world split.

In an instant she saw the dream again the mountain fire, the heat of his body, his lips on hers, the shattering quake of their kiss. For a heartbeat it was not battle but belonging, his stone fingers trembling as though he remembered too.

Her chest ached. She should fear him. And yet she did not.

Karnath's grip slackened. His amber eyes flickered, torn.

"Let her go!" Ragnar's roar shattered the moment. With one brutal swing, he leapt and drove his axe clean through Karnath's neck.

Stone cracked.

The giant's head fell, shattering against the cobblestones. His body dissolved into a cloud of dust and gravel, collapsing into nothing.

Polyonymous fell to her knees, coughing in the haze, her body shaking. Ragnar was there in an instant, pulling her into his arms, his chest heaving.

"It is done," he said, voice ragged.

But Polyonymous stared at the pile of ash

where amber eyes had been. Her lips still burned with the memory of stone.

22

And in her heart, she knew it was not done at all.

Interlude 2 – The Tidal Prince & The Shadowbound

The sea was not calm.

It rose like a beast in the night, waves clawing at the sky, dragging the moonlight into the depths. Polyonymous drifted, bare feet brushing the surface as if it were glass, her gown of silver threads clinging damp to her thighs.

From the foam, he came.

The Tidal Prince, hair dark as kelp, skin sheened with salt, eyes glowing with a pale aquamarine that cut through the storm. His trident shimmered with lightning. "You are far from shore, dreamer," he said, voice breaking like surf against cliffs.

She should have fled. But the sea wrapped her

ankles, tugging her toward him.

Then the air bent behind her.

The Shadowbound emerged horns curved, hair like spilled ink, armour glistening like obsidian wet with blood. His eyes burned, not blue but black fire, watching her as though she already belonged to him. Shadows curled around her waist like hands, possessive, unyielding.

"You cannot claim what does not want you," the prince snarled, striking the sea with his trident. Lightning cracked, waves surging higher.

"And yet," the Shadow whispered, his lips grazing her ear though he stood an arm's length away, "she comes to me."

Her body betrayed her. She reached for both,

the salt of the prince's chest under her palm, the heat of the Shadow's clawed gauntlet against her hip. They pressed closer, the storm and the dark colliding around her. Water drenched her, shadow consumed her, and in that impossible union of sea and night she felt herself breaking, gasping, alive.

Their mouths claimed her in turn salt and storm, fire and night. She was devoured, worshipped, unmade.

But even as the dream deepened, she knew it was not theirs alone.
The Sea Witch was watching.
And she was smiling.

Chapter Five – Salt on Her Skin

Polyonymous's eyes snapped open.

Not to the furs of her chamber. Not to Ragnar's
warmth at her back.
But to cold marble, slick with seawater.

She was sprawled upon the floor of a vast hall,
its pillars shaped like crashing waves, its
windows open to the endless ocean. The air
reeked of brine and storm. And high above,
banners of black and silver rippled, marked
with horns and tridents entwined.

The castle of the dream princes.

Her breath hitched. This was no dream.

From the shadows, whispers echoed, curling
against her skin like wet fingers. A laugh, low

and cruel, slid across the stone. "Run, dreamer," it murmured. "The Sea Witch watches."

Heart hammering, Polyonymous scrambled to her feet. She slipped barefoot through the hall, skirts clinging damp against her legs. Somewhere, the crash of waves grew louder, as though the sea itself followed her.

She reached a balcony that jutted over the black water and gasped. Rising from the depths, barnacle-crusted, scarred from centuries of war, was a dragon. Its scales shimmered with seaweed green and moonlight silver, its eyes glowing with the wisdom of tides older than gods.

"Child of many names," the sea dragon rumbled, voice rolling like distant thunder. "The Witch would bind you. But the sea remembers those who resist."

It lowered its vast head, offering the ridge of its snout. Trembling, Polyonymous climbed astride. With a heave of its wings, the dragon tore from the ocean, droplets scattering like shattered stars.

They soared across night and storm until the coastline of her own kingdom broke through the mist. The dragon dipped low, setting her down just beyond the longhouse gates.

"Beware the Witch," it whispered. "She plays with threads that bind more than dreams." Then it plunged back into the waves and was gone.

Polyonymous crept inside, her gown heavy with salt, her hair damp and tangled. She thought she could slip into her chamber unnoticed until a chirping growl betrayed her.

Dreki.

The little dragon bounded forward, tail wagging, tongue lolling. He pressed his wet snout against her gown, then sneezed spraying her with slobber and smoke. The noise echoed down the hall like a war horn.

"Oh no, you little traitor," she hissed, trying to hush him.

Too late.

"Polyonymous?" Ragnar's voice thundered from the chamber, rough with sleep. "Where have you gone at this hour?"

She froze as he strode into view, bare-chested, hair tangled, eyes narrowing at the sight of her damp gown. He pulled her back into the chamber with one sweep of his arm, scowling.

"You smell of salt," he growled, pressing his forehead to hers. "Not of hearth, nor of me. Of the sea."

Polyonymous swallowed hard, forcing a laugh. "Perhaps Dreki drooled too much again."

Ragnar eyed her, suspicion flickering beneath his tenderness. He pulled her down into the furs, caging her with his warmth. "Wife, I'll not have you slipping from me into the dark."

She pressed her face to his chest, heart still racing. And though she laughed softly against his skin, she could not shake the taste of salt still burning on her lips.

Chapter Six – Steel and Sobs

The clang of weapons rang through the training yard like thunder. Sunlight flashed off steel, sparks flying with each furious strike. Ragnar swung his axe in a wide arc, bellowing as though he fought an army of giants.

"Come at me, beast!" he roared.

Bjorn, chief of his armies, stepped forward. Half man, half bull, the Minotaur towered over the other soldiers. His horns glinted in the morning light; his great hammer poised in one hand. "You are my king," he rumbled, "but your stance is sloppy."

Ragnar charged anyway. Axe met hammer in an explosion of sound. The soldiers cheered, some wincing as the ground itself seemed to shake under their blows.

"Is this all you've got, Bjorn?" Ragnar bellowed, sweat spraying as he swung.

Bjorn snorted. "I'm holding back so you don't cry again."

"I *never* cry!" Ragnar snapped, slamming his axe down.

Bjorn twisted, caught him off balance, and with a casual shove sent Ragnar sprawling face-first into the dirt.

The yard fell silent.

Ragnar groaned, pushed himself up and burst into tears. "She's slipping from me!" he wailed, pounding his fist into the ground. "My queen, my sun, my stars she feels distant, and I do not know why!"
Bjorn blinked, hammer resting on his shoulder.

"We are… still training, yes?"

Ragnar staggered to his feet, tears streaking through the dirt on his face. Then, with no warning, he roared again, swinging wildly. "Fight me, Bjorn! If I cannot hold my wife, I will at least hold my axe!"

Steel clashed. Sparks flew. The soldiers exchanged glances, muttering bets on whether their king would collapse sobbing or fight until his arms fell off.

And true to form, Ragnar did both. He struck furiously one moment, collapsed against Bjorn's chest the next, sobbing into the Minotaur's fur. "She was given to me," he wept. "Gifted by her people. A bride of strange destiny. And yet what if she was never truly mine?"

Bjorn patted him awkwardly on the back with a hand the size of a shield. "There, there. Perhaps she is simply busy."

Ragnar shoved him away, eyes blazing, axe spinning back into motion. "Busy plotting with shadows and storms! I can feel it, Bjorn, like a hook dragging her soul away from me!"

The soldiers ducked as his axe flew past one's head, embedding in a post. Ragnar ripped it free, panting, chest heaving, eyes wild with fury and grief.

Bjorn, steady as a mountain, tilted his horned head. "Then fight harder, my king. Not me. Not the air. Fight for her."

Ragnar froze, breathing ragged. His axe slipped from his fingers, landing in the dirt.

And for once, he did not weep or rage. He only whispered, "I would die a thousand deaths before I let her be taken."

The yard was silent.

Then Dreki bounded in, tail wagging, tongue lolling, and promptly knocked Ragnar flat again, slobbering over his face.

The soldiers roared with laughter.

"See?" Bjorn said, lips twitching. "At least one creature is loyal."

Ragnar shoved the dragonling off and lay in the dirt, arms spread, tears and laughter mixing on his face. "By Odin's hairy balls, Bjorn I am both blessed and cursed."

Chapter Seven – The Stone Battle Table

Torches flared in the longhouse, their smoke curling against beams blackened with age. At the heart of the chamber sat the stone table carved from a single slab of mountain granite, its surface etched with runes and maps of the realms. Around it gathered the lords of Ragnar's people, warriors and jarls, their voices low and sharp as steel.

Ragnar sat at the head, broad shoulders cloaked in furs, his axe resting across his lap. Beside him, Polyonymous wore a mantle of wolfskin, her eyes bright with the same fire as the warriors. Bjorn loomed at her other side, his horns casting shadows over the table, the Minotaur silent but vigilant.

One of the jarls slammed his fist against the

stone. "Our people grow hungry. The mountain passes yield little. We must seize the Riverlands."

Another shook his head. "The Riverlands are fertile, but their lords bend knee to no king. It would bleed us for years."

Bjorn's deep voice rumbled. "Better the coastal fortresses. Control the sea routes, and food flows to us without siege."

Ragnar leaned forward, knuckles white on the haft of his axe. "We will not crawl like beggars, waiting on scraps. We take what is ours. We take *all*. From mountains to seas, from forests to fields. Let the realms remember the roar of Ragnar's people."

The men cheered, striking fists to chests, their cries shaking the rafters.

But Polyonymous raised her hand. The hall quieted. "Glory is sweet, but glory does not feed children. Strike where you can hold. Seize what you can sow. A kingdom built only on blood cannot endure."

Her words settled like snow. For a moment, even Ragnar's chest stilled. Then slowly, he nodded. "A queen's wisdom is sharper than any blade."

The council bent their heads in respect. Plans unfolded river raids, fortress sieges, alliances sealed in steel and fire. The table rang with the promise of conquest, maps marked with blood-red lines of ambition.

When at last the hour grew late, Polyonymous rose. She leaned down, pressing her lips to Ragnar's temple, her hand warm on his jaw. "Good night, my king," she whispered, soft enough for only him to hear.

His eyes followed her as she slipped from the
hall, her shadow trailing along the torchlit
stone. Alone with his jarls, Ragnar spread his
hands over the map. The fire in his gaze
burned brighter than the flames in the hearth.

And Polyonymous, climbing the steps to their
chamber, felt the pull of sleep like a tide.
The dreams were waiting.

Interlude 3 – Huldra, the Elf King of Verdant Light

The forest shimmered like a dream spun of dawn. Sunlight spilled through emerald leaves, turning the air to gold. Polyonymous stepped barefoot onto moss soft as silk, her breath catching at the sight of a kingdom grown, not built castles shaped from trees, bridges woven of living vines, blossoms glowing like stars in the branches.

And then she saw him.

The Elf King Huldra.

Tall and golden, his chest bare beneath runed bronze, his hair falling in sunlit waves. Wings of green fire unfolded behind him, vast and iridescent. His eyes bright, mischievous, eternal fixed on her with the kind of delight that unmoored her soul.

"Dreamer," he said, voice like laughter wrapped in song. "You've walked through fire and shadow. Now walk with me in the light."

He bent, offering his hand, and when she placed hers in his, the forest itself seemed to sigh. The air sang with fairies perched in the branches, their wings buzzing in harmony as he lifted her onto his broad shoulders like she weighed nothing at all.

She laughed, the sound breaking free like sunlight through clouds, as Huldra carried her through his realm. Blossoms fell around them, butterflies chasing in their wake. Every glance he gave her was a promise of joy, of freedom, of passion unburdened by war.

"Stay," he whispered, pausing beneath a

towering oak whose roots pulsed with ancient magic. "Forget kings of stone and seas of shadow. Here, you are not bound by crown or chain. You are only you. And you are mine."

His lips brushed her knee, her thigh, her hand in his. The forest bloomed brighter, vines curling to embrace them, petals falling in a storm of colour. She bent to him, laughter giving way to hunger, and his kiss was green fire wild, alive, and utterly consuming.

For the first time in her dream-journeys, she felt weightless. Not torn. Not cursed. Only wanted.

And as the fairy songs rose to a crescendo, she wondered if dawn would ever let her go.

Chapter Eight – The Valkyrie Ships

The docks thundered with life. Black waves slapped against the wooden piers as men and women hauled ropes, sharpened blades, and stacked barrels of salted meat and mead. The Valkyrie ships stood proud sleek and sharp, their dragon-prowed bows biting the wind, sails stitched with runes of conquest.

"Faster!" Ragnar bellowed, his voice carrying over the clang of hammers and the creak of ropes. "If we don't set sail by dusk, the sea itself will laugh at us!"

Among the chaos, Dreki caused his own storm. The young dragon bounded along the pier, wings flapping wildly, his tail sweeping barrels of apples into the sea. He stuck his snout into a basket of dried fish, sneezed, and set three sailors' tunics smouldering with flame.

"Gods above!" one of them shrieked, slapping at the sparks. "Somebody control that beast!"

Dreki hiccupped, sending another puff of smoke into a warrior's face. The man coughed, staggering blind into the water.

The dock erupted with laughter and curses.

Ragnar stomped forward, scruffing the dragon by the neck with one massive hand. Dreki wriggled, wings drooping guiltily, tongue lolling out as if he'd done no wrong.

"Listen here, little fire hazard," Ragnar growled, holding him nose-to-nose. "You behave on my ship, or by Odin's hairy balls we'll all be floating again like last time."

The soldiers chuckled. Everyone knew the tale: Ragnar's flagship had once burned to its ribs mid-voyage, forcing the crew to cling to driftwood for half a day before rescue.

"I will not float in the sea for twelve hours again!" Ragnar snapped, setting the dragon down. "Do you hear me?"

Dreki wagged his tail and belched smoke directly in his beard.

The dock roared with laughter. Ragnar groaned, muttering, "Cursed beast," but his hand scratched behind Dreki's ear anyway, gentle despite his words.

Meanwhile, Polyonymous stood tall upon the prow of her own Valkyrie ship, the wolfskin mantle sweeping across her shoulders, hair braided with silver and bone. Beside her, Bjorn loomed like a wall of horn and muscle, his great hammer slung at his back.

At Ragnar's order, she would lead the fleet into the waves a queen at the head of war.

Bjorn's deep voice rumbled low. "The king is restless. He feels you slipping, though he does not say it before others. He asked me to watch you. To… remind you, you are not alone."

Polyonymous kept her gaze on the horizon, where the sun bled red against the water. "I thank you, Bjorn. Truly. But I am fine. Ragnar need not worry."

"Still," the Minotaur murmured, "I see his fear. It breaks him more than battle wounds."

She turned at last, meeting his dark, steady eyes. "Then let us win glory swiftly, so his heart rests easy."

Bjorn bowed his great head, satisfied.

With a cry, the war horns blared. Sails unfurled. The Valkyrie ships lurched against the tide, ready to break free from shore.

And at their head, Polyonymous stood her hand steady on the railing, her chin lifted, the queen of Ragnar's fleet.

The sea was waiting.

Chapter Nine – The Queen of Riverlands

The forest burned with war.

Axes crashed against shields, arrows hissed through the air, and the thunder of boots shook the mossy earth. Valkyrie ships had carried Ragnar's people across the waves, and now their banners of dragon snapped above the carnage.

Polyonymous strode through the chaos like a storm made flesh. Blood spattered her furs, her braid whipping as her sword cut through enemy lines. A jarl lunged at her with a spear she wrenched it aside, slammed her blade through his chest, and stepped over his collapsing body without breaking stride.

Bjorn's hammer crashed beside her, sending

three men flying into the trees. "The queen clears her own path," he bellowed, proud.

She roared back, voice carrying above the din. "For Ragnar! For the realm!"

The tide of battle surged and broke and then the noise fell away.

Across the blood-soaked clearing, standing tall among his warriors, was Huldra. The Elf King. Wings of green fire shimmered faintly at his back, though tattered now, stained with ash. His golden hair caught the light, his eyes blazing with the same hunger that burned in her veins.

Polyonymous froze, her chest aching. She still felt him his touch, his kiss, the laughter of his dream-realm. And by the flare in his gaze, she knew he felt her too.

Their warriors hesitated, watching as king and queen locked eyes.

Huldra stepped forward, sword dripping. "Dreamer," he said, voice rough with war and want. "You ask me not to fight, yet you march with an army to tear down my forests."

Her grip tightened on her blade. "We need your lands. Your rivers, your food. Do not make me kill you, Huldra."

He laughed bitterly, pain flashing in his eyes. "And the alternative? I am a king. I bow to no one."

Her voice cut sharp as steel. "Bow to me. Not as my enemy, but as my queen's vow. Supply us with what we need, and we join our clans as one. You remain king here. But I am your queen now and you answer to me. The bloodshed ends here."

The forest held its breath.

Huldra dropped his sword. In two strides he was before her, seizing her in his arms so fiercely she thought he meant to break her. Instead, his mouth crashed against hers, a kiss wild and desperate, filled with all the longing of battle and dream.

When he pulled back, his chest heaved. Then he fell to one knee at her feet.

"Then so it shall be," he said hoarsely. "The Riverlands bend to their queen."

A stunned silence fell across the clearing. Then the forest warriors lowered their blades, voices rising in cries of surrender and oath.

Together, Polyonymous and Huldra walked through the broken field toward Ragnar. The Viking king stood bloodied but unbowed, axe dripping. His men tensed as Huldra approached but when the Elf King knelt before Polyonymous once more, Ragnar's eyes narrowed, then blazed with fierce pride.

"The battle ends," Polyonymous declared, her voice carrying over the field. "The Riverlands are mine. Their people will serve. Their king bows to me."

A roar shook the heavens Vikings, elves, even Bjorn striking his hammer against the earth in salute.

The bloodshed was over. And a new queen had claimed her realm.

Interlude 4 – The Sea King's Warning

The oars still dripped blood and brine when Polyonymous fell into sleep. Her body ached with battle, her furs heavy, the rocking of the Valkyrie ship pulling her under.

And then she was no longer on the ship.

She was in the sea.

Rain lashed her skin, lightning split the sky, and waves rose around her like walls. The water clung to her body as though alive, dragging her deeper until she stood waist-deep in a black tide.

From the storm, he came.

The Sea King horns curling like coral, his beard

tangled with kelp, his chest ridged and scarred like cliffs beaten by centuries of waves. His eyes glowed with a light older than the moon, and when he touched her cheek with his wet, calloused hand, her breath caught.

"You are pulled to us," he rumbled, voice like thunder rolling through caverns. "Kings of stone, kings of forest, kings of shadow… and now the sea. You cannot resist."

Polyonymous pressed her palm against his chest, trembling at the heat beneath the salt and storm. "I don't choose this. I only dream and each time, I wake with another chain on my heart."

His mouth brushed hers, tasting of salt and storm. "And yet… you do not turn away."

Her chest ached. She could not. The kiss

deepened, crushing and fierce, her body
arching into his as the sea itself roared. It was
not gentle it was claiming, demanding,
irresistible.

When he pulled back, his forehead pressed to
hers, his breath harsh. "The dreams are not
your prison. They are your map. If you would
live, if you would rule, you must seek the one
who weaves these tides together."

"The Sea Witch," she whispered.

His grip tightened at her waist. "Yes. But
beware, dreamer"

A horn blared.

Her eyes flew open to shouting, boots
thundering on deck, the creak of ropes. "Land!
We've made land!"

The dream dissolved, the Sea King's warning
lost to the storm as daylight dragged her back.

And though the ship rocked steady beneath
her, Polyonymous's skin still burned with salt
and the press of his lips.

Chapter Ten – Thunder in Her Veins

The great hall buzzed with whispers. Servants bent low, but their eyes darted like crows, and the warriors at the long tables spoke in low voices that carried far enough for all to hear.

They spoke of the battle in the Riverlands.
They spoke of victory.
But most of all, they spoke of the kiss.

The kiss between their queen and the Elf King.

Ragnar ignored it at first. He poured Polyonymous mead at feasts, pulled her onto his knee before the jarls, showered her with furs and jewels, with the weight of his hand at her hip and the press of his lips at her temple. But the more he tried, the more she slipped from him her eyes turned away, her laugh hollow, her warmth gone cold.

Finally, his temper broke.

He found her in their chamber, standing before the fire, braiding her hair with a distracted hand. The gossip burned in his skull, the ache in his chest sharper than any wound.

"Tell me it is lies," he demanded, his voice low, trembling with rage. "Tell me you did not kiss him."

Polyonymous turned, her face calm, almost too calm. "It was nothing but gossip, Ragnar. Leave it."

"Gossip?" His laugh cracked like ice. "The hall hums with it. My men my people speak of their queen and another king, and you say leave it?"

She lifted her chin. "I am yours. That is all you need know."

But he stepped closer, eyes blazing. "No. You pull away when I touch you. You hide your eyes when I say I love you. What is happening to you, Polyonymous? What are you hiding from me?"

Her lips trembled. "Nothing."

"Lies!" His roar shook the chamber.

Her own anger surged to meet it, hot and violent. She reached beneath her mantle, pulling free the hammer she had kept hidden the gift, the curse, the inheritance whispered in her blood. Mjölnir.

The chamber went still. Ragnar's eyes widened, his breath caught.

"Do not press me further," she hissed, her voice low and shaking.

But he did. "What are you?"

Her fury broke. She swung the hammer against the wall.

Lightning exploded. The stone shattered, a blinding flash splitting the air, the roar of thunder collapsing the chamber's side into rubble. Servants screamed, warriors staggered, smoke and dust filled the hall.

Ragnar stood frozen, eyes wide, face pale, the crackling glow of lightning still sparking across her shoulders.

And Polyonymous, chest heaving, tears burning her eyes, turned and fled into the storm outside.

Chapter Eleven – The Cave by the Sea

The storm had passed, leaving the sky bruised purple, the ocean below restless and dark. At the edge of the cliffs, hidden in the crags of stone, a small cave opened onto a view that stretched forever sea and land bound together beneath the fading light.

It was there Ragnar found her.

Polyonymous sat curled on a ledge, her knees drawn to her chest, the salt wind in her hair. Dreki lay at her feet, tail thumping gently against the stone, as though guarding her from grief itself.

Ragnar's boots crunched softly as he entered. He paused, his broad shoulders filling the cave mouth, then gave a nervous laugh. "So…

thunder and lightning bolts." He scratched his beard. "That was new."

Polyonymous didn't look at him.

Ragnar stepped closer, lowering himself to sit beside her. "I suppose I'll need to behave myself from now on. Wouldn't want you to blow up our whole castle over a quarrel, eh?" He bumped her shoulder playfully, a crooked smile tugging at his lips.

A reluctant laugh slipped from her throat. "Perhaps you should."

"There she is," he said warmly, wrapping his arm around her. He pulled her against his chest, pressing his face into her hair. "My storm queen."

For a while they sat in silence, watching the

waves. Dreki snored softly, smoke curling from his nostrils, his little claws twitching in dreams.

Then Ragnar shifted, fingers finding her side. He tickled her lightly, and she squealed, swatting at his hand. "Ragnar!"

He grinned, unrepentant. "I thought perhaps the thunder might return if I poked the right spot."
She giggled despite herself, twisting to face him, her laughter fading into a sigh. "I don't know what's happening to me, Ragnar. These dreams… this power… I can't control it."

He cupped her face, his thumb brushing her cheek. "Then we learn together."

She searched his eyes, her voice low. "Tell me again… about the ones who gave me to you.

Why did they choose me as queen? What did they know that I don't?"

Ragnar's jaw tightened. He looked away, out to the sea, the wind pulling at his hair. "I was told you were… important. Precious to your people. A gift beyond measure. But now…" He shook his head slowly. "Now I see they told me only half the truth."

Her breath caught. "So, you suspect more?"

He met her gaze again, his expression heavy with both love and fear. "Aye. You are more than queen. More than wife. You are something the realms have been waiting for."

The waves crashed below, lightning flickering faint on the horizon. And Polyonymous, nestled against him, felt the weight of destiny pressing harder than ever.

Interlude 5: The Child and the Storm

The dream did not carry her into the arms of another realm's lover this time. Instead, Polyonymous awoke inside the dream standing in a vast storm-lit hall. The walls were carved of black stone that seemed alive with veins of lightning, sparking and dancing across the surface as if the whole structure breathed the storm. Above her, a ceiling of churning thunderclouds cracked open with flashes of silver fire. Her body hummed with energy, threads of lightning weaving across her skin until she appeared as though she herself had been forged from the storm's heart.

In her hands she gripped two blades of living light.

They vibrated with the weight of thunder, their edges alive with sparks that hissed when they touched the ground. She looked down at herself, her gown transformed into a storm-draped garment that shimmered with every flicker of the lightning. It felt powerful wild and raw but also frightening, as though the storm were testing her, and she was only beginning to understand its rules.

At the far end of the hall sat a boy upon a throne.

He looked no older than twelve, his small frame dwarfed by the great chair carved from ancient stone. Yet despite his youth, he sat with a regal posture, his hands resting easily on the armrests as though the throne had always been his. His hair was a tumble of curls, his eyes sharp with a wisdom that did not belong to a child. Behind him loomed a dragon, scales the colour of iron, eyes burning gold.

Its wings folded neatly, but its presence filled the chamber with a suffocating gravity, as if to remind her that it could destroy everything in an instant.

The boy's gaze fixed on her, and when he spoke, his voice rang with clarity that cut through the thunder:

"Someday all this will be mine. Someday, it may be yours too."

Polyonymous tilted her head, the lightning crackling brighter around her shoulders like a living veil. "Yours? Who are you to claim such a hall?"

The boy leaned forward, the faintest flicker of amusement in his eyes, as though he enjoyed keeping her guessing. "My name is"

Thunder cracked. The hall convulsed, lightning pouring down in jagged rivers of white and blue.

The throne, the dragon, and the boy dissolved into shards of stormlight before the final word could leave his lips.

Polyonymous jolted awake, her chest heaving. Ragnar's voice was calling her name, sharp and urgent, pulling her from the dream.

Chapter Twelve: The Lights of the North

"Polyonymous."

Ragnar's voice pulled her out of the dream before the boy could finish his name. Her heart still hammered, the storm echoing in her chest. She sat up, blinking, the heat of phantom lightning still in her palms.

Ragnar leaned over her, his smile faintly crooked, his eyes bright with mischief. "Come, little thunder heart. I did not wake you to watch you sweat and thrash about like a berserker in your sleep. There is something better outside worth the loss of dreams, even ones that make you curse in your tongue."

She scowled faintly. "I was not thrashing."

"Oh no, of course not," Ragnar teased, lifting an eyebrow. "The wall you nearly scorched in your sleep was simply trembling out of respect."

Despite the heat in her cheeks, she laughed, and the sound loosened the last grip of the storm. Ragnar took her hand and drew her out into the night.

The sky opened above them in ribbons of fire and frost. Curtains of emerald, sapphire, and violet rippled from horizon to horizon the northern lights, alive, moving, shifting as if some gods were painting them in real time. Beneath their glow, Ragnar had built a fire on the cliff's edge. Its flames snapped and danced, the warmth pushing back the chill air rolling in from the sea.

"See?" Ragnar whispered, pulling her against

his chest. "The heavens are showing off for us. Even they cannot resist your storm."

The words made her blush, but he tightened his hold and pressed his forehead to hers. His beard brushed her skin, rough and tender all at once. She could smell smoke and salt on him, and beneath that, the warmth that was wholly Ragnar.

They sank to the ground together, the fire crackling at their side, its light painting their faces in gold. The aurora spread like wings above them. For a long while, they said nothing, only holding each other, letting the silence roar with the same intensity as any storm.

Finally, he spoke, softer now: "You were dreaming. I could see it in your eyes when I woke you. What haunted you, thunder heart?"

Polyonymous hesitated. "A boy. A hall made of storm and stone. He said it would all be his one day. He almost told me his name… but the dream broke apart before he did."

Ragnar froze, then let out a laugh that boomed louder than the fire. "So, what was he going to say? Goat-boy? Little Thor still in swaddling?"

She swatted at him, but her lips curved despite herself. "I'm serious, Ragnar. It felt real."

His grin softened, though the humour lingered in his eyes. "Dreams love to play tricks. If it felt real, perhaps the Norns wanted you restless. But I'll not have them steal you from this night."

He kissed her hair, pulling her closer. "Leave the dreams to the dream weavers. The sky has gifted us fire and colour and I'll not let you waste it brooding over some boy who could not even finish his name."

Her protest faded when his lips found hers. What began as gentle turned fierce, passion igniting like sparks from the fire. He drew her into his lap, his hands anchoring her as though he feared she might slip back into that storm and be lost to him. She clung to him, her laughter breaking between kisses until the night itself seemed to pulse with their heat.

Above them, the aurora flared brighter, curtains of green and violet sweeping across the heavens as though the gods themselves leaned in to watch. By the fire's glow, two shadows merged into one, their laughter and passion twining with the crackle of flame and the song of the northern lights.

Chapter Thirteen: The Brothers Under the Lights

The fire had burned low, embers glowing faint beneath the northern sky. Ragnar's arm wrapped heavy and warm around Polyonymous as she drifted between dream and waking, her cheek pressed to the rise of his chest. His breathing was steady, his weight grounding her after the chaos of the storm-dream. For the first time in days, she felt safe.

That illusion shattered in an instant.

Boots pounded the snow. Harsh voices barked orders in the night. The sudden ring of steel sang out as shadows closed around them. Before she could react, a rough hand seized her wrist, yanking her from Ragnar's embrace. Polyonymous cried out, but her voice was cut short as coarse fabric was dragged over her head. Darkness swallowed her, muffling her breath. Shackles clamped tight around her wrists before she could summon lightning. Her swords were gone, stripped away by practiced hands.

Beside her, Ragnar roared in fury, the sound guttural, savage. She heard the clash of steel as he fought, but the fight was short-lived. The sound of armoured men overwhelming him ended in a grunt of pain and the snap of iron binding his arms.

"Ragnar!" Polyonymous struggled, but a soldier shoved her forward, sending her stumbling into the snow. Rough hands held her upright as she fought, dragged across the frozen ground. The warmth of the fire vanished behind them, its glow swallowed by the dark.

The world became motion and sound: boots crunching on snow, armour rattling in rhythm, and muffled curses from Ragnar somewhere close. Cold air seared her lungs, the night vast and merciless around them. Though the hood over her face robbed her of sight, she could feel the path beneath her shifting snow giving way to frozen earth, earth giving way to cobblestones.

They marched for what felt like hours. The sound of torches hissed and spat in the wind. Every stumble earned her a shove, every hesitation, a barked order in a voice she did not recognize. Her wrists ached beneath the shackles, her shoulders straining as she was forced onward. Yet she kept listening for Ragnar's voice, for any clue of escape. He was still there, his presence undeniable, his growling defiance answering every insult hurled at them.

At last, a deep groan of iron split the night the sound of gates opening. The march slowed as they crossed into a place where echoes bounced off walls. The air shifted, warmer now, carrying the faint smell of smoke and stone. Boots thudded hollow against a floor of worked stone. She felt the air change again as they entered a hall vast enough to swallow the world.

With a sudden jerk, the hood was ripped from her head. Polyonymous blinked, her eyes stinging in the torchlight. Ragnar stood shackled beside her, his face smeared with frost and fury. Before them sprawled a great hall, its ceiling lost in shadow. Torches lined the walls, and fire pits burned in wide stone braziers, their flames chasing the cold from the chamber.

At the far end sat a man who could have been

Ragnar's reflection in another life. His hair was raven-dark, his eyes storm-bright blue, glinting with calculation. A cloak trimmed in fur draped across his broad shoulders, and a black leather jerkin bore the emblem of a silver stag. He lounged in a high-backed chair with the ease of one accustomed to command.

Ragnar's face shifted from fury to shock. Then, with a bark of laughter that echoed through the hall, he cried, "By Odin's balls! I thought we'd been taken by the enemy!"

The man rose, a grin cutting sharp across his face. "Brother."

Ragnar strained against his chains before his captors could stop him. But the man lifted a hand, and the soldiers stepped back. The two men closed the distance, crashing together in an embrace that rattled bone. Their laughter rolled through the hall, their arms locked in the bone-crushing grip of warriors testing each other's strength.

"Hymir," Ragnar said at last, voice booming with joy. "Still ruling your corner of the world with iron and antlers, I see."

Hymir pulled back just enough to glance at Polyonymous. His storm-bright eyes softened as they fell upon her. "And you would sneak into my lands," he said, grin widening, "and deny me the honour of meeting your beautiful queen?"

Polyonymous, still breathless from the capture, blinked in surprise. Ragnar puffed his chest proudly, keeping her tucked at his side. "I would deny you nothing, brother. Only a fool would try."

Hymir laughed, the sound rolling like thunder. "Then tell me, why were the two of you sleeping in the snow like beggars, when you could have been warm within walls?"

Ragnar's lips twitched with mischief. "Ah. A little mishap. My thunderheart here decided to test the strength of stone walls with lightning. The chamber lost. I thought it safer not to risk your castle before repairs could be made."

Polyonymous groaned, covering her face, but both brothers roared with laughter. Hymir clapped Ragnar's back hard enough to stagger him.

"Then you will stay with me," Hymir declared. His voice filled the hall, carrying the weight of command. "I insist. We will feast, we will drink, and we will talk of lands and war. Too long has it been since we spoke as brothers."

At his command, servants rushed to prepare the hall. Long tables were laden with roasted meats, bread fresh from the hearth, wheels of cheese, and casks of mead. Candles and torches flared brighter as though the hall itself came alive. Musicians began to tune harps and lutes in the corner, their notes carrying above the hum of activity.

Polyonymous sank into a seat beside Ragnar as their shackles were finally struck off. Her wrists ached, but the warmth of the fire and the sight of Ragnar and Hymir laughing together eased the lingering terror. The air was thick with the scent of roasting venison, spiced ale, and woodsmoke. Silver cups were filled, and platters passed until no space on the tables remained bare.

Ragnar raised his horn high. "To brothers, to queens, and to nights stolen back from fear!"

The hall erupted in cheers, the sound rising to meet the vaulted ceiling. Hymir leaned close, his voice low and full of promise. "Stay, brother. Stay, and let us speak of more than feasting. Let us speak of lands, of strength, of a future we might carve together."

Polyonymous watched the firelight dance across both men's faces. The night of terror in the snow had shifted into a new storm one of ambition, reunion, and unspoken danger.

Chapter Fourteen: The Brothers Under the Lights – The Banquet

The hall thundered with cheer as servants poured mead into silver horns, and the scent of roasted venison, juniper, and woodsmoke wove through the air. Long banners with the silver stag hung from the rafters, their cloth stirring in the heat that rose from the braziers.

Laughter rolled like surf against rock, steady and bright, and the minstrel by the hearth plucked at his lute with the patience of a fisherman waiting for the tide. The music was a thread through the noise, thin and sure, tying the room together.

Ragnar leaned back on the carved oaken bench, his posture loose, eyes alight. He was already halfway through his second horn, and his cheeks were warmed the colour of sunrise. "By the gods, Hymir, you have grown soft," he said, grinning. "The man I remember ate with his hands and wiped his beard on his sleeve. Now look at you, banners, silver plates, boots that shine like river stones."

Hymir tipped his horn in mock courtesy. "And yet here you sit, brother, drinking from my horn and dirtying my silver. Tell me, has your thunderheart grown so mighty she can bring down walls, yet cannot conjure a bed from sea mist and moonlight."

The table roared. Polyonymous pressed her lips together to hold back a smile. Ragnar's arm curled around her shoulder and tugged her close. He kissed her hair, then spoke to the hall. "She tested the stones; the stones failed the test. I thought it kinder to spare Hymir's hall while we wait for our own to be mended."

Hymir laughed and slapped the table with a sound like a drum. "Then I owe your queen my gratitude. If she is to test my walls, let it be with song and not with storm." He stood and raised his horn. "To Polyonymous, breaker of poor masonry, keeper of Ragnar's temper, light in these northern nights."

Cups rose in answer. Polyonymous flushed, then nodded, surprised at the warmth that met her. She felt the room take her in and weigh her, curious, not unkind. The firelight put copper on Ragnar's beard and stars in Hymir's eyes. She breathed in, and the scent of honeyed ale and pine helped steady the last tremor left by the ambush.

A platter of boar slid down the table. Ragnar carved with a hunter's ease, handing Polyonymous the first slice. Hymir watched the motion with a quiet satisfaction only brothers could read. When the plates were filled, he leaned forward, elbows on the table, voice pitched for the room yet meant for the two of them.

"It has been too long," Hymir said. "Too many winters where I counted my neighbours like wolves count deer. We have strength, you and I, and the world grows hungry. Together we could hold the passes and the river mouths. The north could be a single shield wall."

Ragnar chewed, then wiped his mouth with the back of his hand. "You always did talk like a captain even when we were children. Do you remember the winter we stole Father's skiff, and you tried to command the tide. The tide paid you no mind, and we came home soaked, and Father laughed until he cried."

Hymir smiled, and the sharpness in him softened. "The tide did as it wished, true, yet I learned to watch it. A man who watches long enough can ride a thing he cannot master. That is what I speak of tonight. Not command, not chains, only timing."
Ragnar's gaze flicked to Polyonymous and back again. "Timing is a pretty word when you ask a brother for his ships."

"And his queen," someone at the far end shouted, the words loose with drink. A few heads turned.

Hymir did not look away from Ragnar, but his grin showed the curve of a fang.

Polyonymous felt the room lean toward them as if the hall itself had ears. She set her knife down and folded her hands, steady. "If I am a piece on a board, then I should like to know the game."

Hymir bowed slightly from where he sat. "No board, my lady, and no pieces. Only a map and two brothers who have not read it together in too many years." He poured more mead and passed the horn to her. "Drink and forgive our sharp edges. Steel honed on steel keeps both blades honest."

Ragnar took the horn from her and drank first, eyes on Hymir over the rim. "He means to say he will not insult you while he is asking for your help."

"I would not insult her in any season," Hymir said, and the room murmured approval. "I would ask her which storms she serves. I would ask if she would help us shape the wind rather than live beneath the weather."

The minstrel shifted keys. The new tune moved like a river under ice, slow and clear. A woman with hair the colour of wheat rose near the hearth and began a soft chorus. Others joined, and soon the hall carried a song that sounded older than the beams that held the roof. Ragnar tapped Polyonymous's hand in time with the rhythm, then leaned close so only she could hear.

"He will talk of maps and watch your eyes," Ragnar murmured. "If you nod in the right places, he will call it fate. If you frown, he will call it a test. He is my brother; he is also a hunter."

She smiled without showing her teeth. "Then let us be two hunters who share the fire, and not the prey who warms it."

Ragnar bit back a laugh. His pride in her shone through him like heat. He raised his voice again.

"Hymir, do you truly plan to take a single step without wrestling me for it first. Or will you try to flatter me into a saddle and call it a throne."

"Oh, I will wrestle you," Hymir said, and stood.

The hall cheered. "But not before we eat like kings." He clapped twice. A line of servants entered with a boar's head crowned in rosemary, a mountain of buttered turnips, dark bread split and steaming, wheels of cheese that bled pale gold onto the boards, bowls of sweetened berries, and casks that sloshed when set down.

Hymir moved around the table and refilled cups himself. He stopped behind Polyonymous and spoke for her ear alone. "You broke a wall to spare a heart. My men speak of it already. They say you woke lightning as if it were a sleeping dog you knew by name."

She kept her gaze on the table and answered low. "Lightning is not a dog. It is a road you can stand on only once."

"Then I thank you for choosing that road near my borders," Hymir said. His tone held no sarcasm. He returned to his chair and lifted his hands. "Now, skald, give us something that smells of salt and steel."

The minstrel obliged. He sang of long keels knifing through black water, of stars that never slept, of shields stacked like roof tiles, and of a woman who walked at the prow with thunder in her hair. The men beat time on the tables with their fists. Ragnar joined with both palms and a grin that split his face.

When the song ended, Ragnar stood and balanced on the bench like a boy. "You forget the verse where the woman at the prow told the captain to stop shouting at waves," he called, and the hall laughed. "You forget the verse where the captain listened." He bowed toward Hymir with a flourish so grand he nearly toppled. "He was a fast learner."

Hymir spread his hands as if to say, what can a man do. "A man listens when the storm speaks sense." He turned serious by a subtle degree. "Ragnar, I speak plainly now. The eastern clans stir, and traders whisper of a banner made of black sun and crooked nails. They are not our kin, and they move like frost moves, quiet and hard. If they come by sea, your ships matter. If they come by land, my walls matter. Together, we could break them at the river neck."

The humour in Ragnar's face cooled, not gone, only banked. "You lead with a jest, you finish with a threat. You have always known how to use both." He set his cup down. "We will talk terms after the feast, and you will not try to sell me my own men with prettier words."

"Agreed," Hymir said. He looked at Polyonymous again. "And you, my lady. Would you give counsel when we speak. I value the mind that can turn lightning aside to spare a life."

Polyonymous felt the pull of the room's attention again, light as a net on the skin. She looked from one brother to the other and saw two boys who had grown into kings without losing the urge to outdo each other. "I will give counsel," she said, "and I will hear the river before I judge it. I am new to these shores. It would be poor manners to move furniture in a hall I have only just entered."

Ragnar laughed softly. Hymir's grin flickered, pleased. A servant placed a small plate by Polyonymous's elbow, sugared berries beside slices of pear, and a wedge of pale cheese that smelled faintly of flowers. She ate, and warmth crawled back into her fingers.

As the night loosened and the casks lowered, the feast tilted toward rowdy. A wrestling match burst to life near the hearth, boots skidding on rushes, the crowd calling bets. A man tried to balance a knife on his nose, failed, and kissed the floor to great acclaim. Hymir told a story about a raider who mistook a priest for a sea witch and apologized for three months. Ragnar topped it with a tale of a goat that stole a king's crown and wore it into battle. The goat survived, and the crown did not.

Polyonymous laughed until her sides ached. Each bout of laughter came with a private memory of the snow, the hood, the ring of iron, and the thought unravelled a little more. She leaned into Ragnar and let the sound of the room mend what fear had frayed. At moments she caught Hymir watching, and his eyes were not cold then. They were the eyes of a man taking measure, and also of a brother remembering he had a brother still.

When the skald began a circle dance, Ragnar stood and offered his hand. "Come, thunderheart," he said. "If we must speak of rivers tomorrow, tonight we will be boats." He led her to the firelight and spun her, gentle at first, then faster as the drum found a quicker beat. She moved like she had been born on a ship, sure on her feet, light in the turn.

The hall clapped time and shouted praise. Hymir watched with a smile that reached his eyes.

The dance ended with laughter and breathless bows. Ragnar guided her back to the bench and pressed his forehead to hers for a heartbeat. "You make every sky look tame," he whispered. She answered with a grin that was almost a challenge. "Then choose a bigger sky."

Hymir raised his horn once more. "To storms that walk, to brothers who live long enough to grow wise, and to the north that will not bow." The response shook the rafters. He sat and lowered his voice. "We meet at dawn, Ragnar. Bring your stubbornness. I will bring mine." Ragnar chuckled. "I will bring Polyonymous. She keeps us both from falling on our swords."

"Then bring her twice," Hymir said, and for a moment the three of them shared a look that felt like a pact, fragile and bright.

Later, when the hall thinned and the last cask slept on its side, Ragnar walked with Polyonymous along the periphery where the torches threw softer light.

The stone was warm beneath their boots, and the draft carried hints of the sea. He linked his fingers with hers. "I know my brother," he said. "He is a cliff the sea cannot help but test. He will not mean you harm, yet he will see what shape you are. If he pushes too hard, say the word, and I will break his nose."

She laughed, quiet and full. "You will not break his nose."

"No," Ragnar admitted, amused. "I will only threaten it until it behaves." He sobered a fraction.

"Are you well."

She considered, then nodded. "I am warm. I am fed.

I am watched by a man who knows the currents. That is as well as a woman can be in a strange hall." She squeezed his hand. "I will sleep, and I will dream of a name that almost found me."

Ragnar brushed a kiss against her temple. "Let the dream come when it will. Tonight, you owe the sky your smile and me your breath."

They returned to the table for one last cup. Hymir raised his in silent salute across the distance.

Polyonymous returned the gesture and felt the thread of the night pull tight, then tie. The feast had not ended the storm. It had only given it a hearth.

Tomorrow would bring maps and terms. Tonight, had brought laughter, bread, and a brother found again.

Interlude 6, The Frost Dream

The dream opened to blue. Blue sky, blue ice, blue shadow. A slow drift of snow like sifted flour fell over the frost lands and collected along the ribs of an ancient glacier. An ice castle rose from it, a cathedral of frozen light, every window a pale lantern. Wind curled through the spires and sang a thin song across the valley.

Polyonymous stood at the arched gate with her hand tucked inside a much larger one. Jötunn, a Jötnar with skin like dusk over snow, watched her with eyes the colour of winter fire. His hair was pale as hoarfrost and long enough to brush the fur collar of his hunting cloak.

"Home," he said, and the word felt like a blanket drawn to her chin.

From the courtyard came a joyous yowl.
Snæbjörn, their snow leopard, bounded
toward them, a massive cloud of white fur
ridged with silver stripes. He pressed his great
head into Polyonymous's stomach and huffed
a warm breath, then stepped to Jötunn and
accepted a scratch beneath his jaw.

"Inside," Polyonymous laughed, "before you
shake snow all over the hall."

Two small bodies shot through the door ahead
of them. Thiassi, six, bright eyed and quick as
ice-sparks, skidded across the polished floor in
her wool socks. Snoer, four, with a grin
missing two teeth, held up a hand-carved
figure of Snæbjörn and announced, very
seriously, "I am training him to be brave."

"He already is," Jötunn said, swooping the boy
up to his shoulder. "But he needs a captain.

That is, you, little storm."

They ate together at a low table carved from river ice, warmed from beneath by hidden stones. Jötunn cracked the seal on a cask of cloudberry wine. Polyonymous tore bread and dipped it in a stew that steamed like breath in cold air. Thiassi told a story about how she had seen the sun catch a snowflake and turn it to a tiny star. Snoer insisted his toy had growled at a drift and scared it away. Snæbjörn sprawled by the hearth with his long tail wrapped neatly around his paws, yellow eyes half closed.

When the plates were stacked and the last of the berries licked from small fingers, they bundled the children into coats and went outside. The night had arrived while they ate, a great velvet bowl hung with green ribbons of aurora. Polyonymous and Jötunn held mittened hands while the children tumbled through shallow powder and Snæbjörn loped around them, careful and proud, his whiskers edged with frost.

"Race you to the snow stairs," Thiassi called.

"Only if Snæbjörn lets you win," Jötunn said, and the great cat chuffed, which made Snoer laugh so hard he fell backward.

Later, after stories and milk sweetened with honey, they tucked the children into a bed that looked like a ship of furs sailing through an ocean of quilts. Polyonymous kissed their foreheads and watched them sink into sleep. Jötunn stood behind her with his hand at her waist.

"They are perfect," she whispered.

"They are," he said.

They walked the quiet corridor where the ice walls carried little glows like held starlight. Inside their chamber the hearthstones sent up a soft warmth. Jötunn unfastened her laces with patient fingers. She traced old scars along his shoulder as if reading a map, then rested her forehead against his. In the hush of the frost lands, they loved each other, slow and certain, the kind of closeness that feels like a vow spoken without words. They slept with their legs tangled, her ear over the steady drum of his heart.

Morning arrived pearly and calm. She woke to Jötunn's arm heavy over her and the distant sound of children whispering in the hall. When they joined them, Thiassi was dressing Snæbjörn in a wreath of pine, very dignified, and Snoer had given the toy leopard a matching twig crown.

"My king," Snoer told the real cat, "you must lead the procession."

Snæbjörn accepted the honour with a tilt of his great head.

Polyonymous laughed and touched Jötunn's cheek. He caught her hand and kissed the heel of her palm.

A crack sounded in the air, small and sharp, like ice struck with iron.

Snæbjörn jerked. For the briefest blink everything was still. Then the cat staggered, a red bloom opening at his shoulder. Thiassi screamed. Snoer froze, toy clutched to his chest. A second crack split the morning, and the wreath toppled to the snow.

"Inside," Jötunn roared. He moved with

impossible speed, sweeping both children into his arms. Another shot ripped the air. Snæbjörn tried to stand. He fell. Polyonymous felt the world tilt.

"Jötunn," she cried, and ran.

Figures moved at the ridge, black specks against the white. One stepped forward. A dark uniform of leather and fur, an antlered deer pin at the breast. She could not see his face, but a shape in the jaw, a way of holding the shoulders, felt like a name spoken behind a door. Hymir. Ragnar's brother. Or a shadow that wore his walk.

"Run," Jötunn said to the children. He turned to face the ridge, arms spreading to make a wall of himself. Thiassi clung to his neck. Snoer wrapped his legs around Jötunn's waist.

The third shot found Jötunn in the back. He grunted, staggered, stayed standing by will alone. Thiassi sobbed, small fingers slipping.

"No," Polyonymous said, the word breaking. She reached, but the fourth shot came like a hammer. Jötunn fell to one knee. The children slid from his arms into the snow. The fifth shot took them both.

The scream that tore from Polyonymous did not sound human. It came from bones and blood and every life she had ever carried in her dreams. She went to her knees, hands in the snow that was suddenly not white at all. Snæbjörn's great flank rose once, then stilled. Thiassi's mitten had a pine needle stuck to it. Snoer's toy lay on its side, its carved mouth open in a forever growl.
Boots crunched closer. The dark figure approached, slow and sure, the deer pin

winking once. Polyonymous could not make out his face. Perhaps the world would not let her.

She lifted her head. The aurora snapped above like a torn ribbon. Somewhere far away horns sounded, low and summoning, as if from another shore. The air she breathed turned thin. The edges of the world went gray.

"Jötunn," she whispered. "My love."

The horns called again, closer, insistent. Hands she could not see seized her shoulders and dragged her backward through a door made of nothing but cold. The ice castle spun away, the ridge, the fallen wreath, the deer pin. She fell.

Polyonymous woke with a gasp in another bed, in another realm, in a room filled with stone and flame. Her throat hurt. Her chest felt cracked. The horns that had pulled her from the dream were echoing across Hymir's fortress, calling all to rise for council at dawn.

Ragnar slept half turned toward her, concern already creasing his brow even in rest. She pressed her fist to her mouth to hold in the new scream trying to climb her spine. Tears slid hot into her hair.

"Was it a dream," she asked the dark, "or is this the dream."

No one answered. Only the horns, and the weight of a loss that felt larger than any world. She lay there with her eyes open, listening to the call to council, and tasted snow that was not here.

Chapter 15, The Ice of Memory

Dawn had the colour of steel. Hymir's men lined the corridor like statues while servants lit torches against a draft that never quite left the bones of the keep. Ragnar found Polyonymous already dressed, boots on, jaw set.

"You did not sleep," he said softly.

"I did," she answered, "once, in a world that was taken from me."

Ragnar searched her face. Something in what he saw made him nod, not in understanding, but in pledge. "Then we will find what can be found."

Hymir entered with the inexhaustible certainty

of a man who thinks the day is already his. The brothers embraced like men who had shared both bread and blood.

Sensing her eyes, Hymir gave Polyonymous a measuring look. "Sister," he said, courteous, cool. "You honour the council."

"I need a different kind of council," she replied. "I need truth."

Ragnar glanced between them. "Hymir, she has questions about your northern campaigns."

Hymir's attention sharpened. "Which campaigns."

"The frost lands," Polyonymous said. The words cost her, but she spent them. "Battles with Jötnar. A captured ice castle. A ridge above a valley. Men in leather and fur. A deer pin, right here." She touched two fingers to the left side of her chest.

Silence pressed the corridor. A spark ticked in a torch.

Hymir tilted his head. "How would you know of that."

"Because I was there," she said. "Because I lived there. Because I loved there. Because that is where I lost everything."

Ragnar's breath left him. Hymir's mouth made a line.

"We have not met before today," Hymir said, careful. "You cannot have been there."

"You led the assault," Polyonymous said. "You

stood on the ridge. Your men took aim."

Hymir's gaze slid to Ragnar. His voice, when it came, was not unkind. "Brother, your wife dreams. She speaks of visions as if they were roads she has walked."

"She does walk them," Ragnar said. "You have not seen what I have seen."

Hymir considered, then gestured. "Come," he said. "There is a place not far. You can tell me if it matches your dream."

They rode beneath a sky that could not decide between blue and white. Frost glazed the pines. Ravens marked their passage with black commas across the air. Hymir led at a steady pace, Ragnar beside Polyonymous, close enough that his knee brushed her boot at every jolt.

They crested a low rise and the land fell away
to a valley shaped like a wide bowl. In its
centre stood an ice castle, thrown up from the
earth as if the ground had exhaled it. The
spires, the narrow windows, the long blue
shadows. Polyonymous's hand tightened on
her reins until the leather creaked.

"We took it in winter two years past," Hymir
said. "Giants had held it. They raided our lines.
We answered."

Polyonymous slid from the saddle. She walked
toward the gate with the determined step of
someone crossing a busy road. Her breath
plumed. The closer she came, the more the air
changed. Something like recognition moved
along her skin, a prickle, a hush.

Inside the courtyard the wind was still. The
stones beneath the ice were familiar under her

boots, a pattern her muscles recalled. She knew where a stair would curl behind a wall. She knew where the corridor would narrow before opening into the low hall with the stones warmed from beneath.

Her fingertips grazed the wall. The ice shone back at her, and in that shine the thinnest ghost of a reflection appeared, then another beside it. Jötunn, his hair a fall of pale light. Thiassi with a pine needle in her braid. Snoer with his carved toy held high. Snæbjörn's whiskers bright with frost. The images rippled and were gone, as if disturbed by a breath.

She closed her eyes. The memory rose around her like water.

Hymir's boots sounded behind her. "This is the place," he said, as if it cost him nothing.
"Tell me," Polyonymous said without turning,

"what you did here."

"We won," Hymir answered. "We cut them from the valley. They fought hard. They always do."

"Tell me everything," she said. "Tell me what you wore. Tell me what you pinned to your chest. Tell me who fired first. Tell me what fell."

Hymir's jaw worked once. He looked at Ragnar, then back. "If I answer, will you hear it as a soldier hears it."

"I will hear it as a mother," she said. "And a wife."

Something in that truth bent Hymir's head a fraction. When he spoke, his voice lost its iron. "We came before dawn," he said. "Snow held the valley. We took the ridge. My scouts reported a family inside, Jötnar blood. A male, a woman, two small ones. A beast the size of a pony. We believed them sentinels. I ordered shots to draw out fighters. The beast fell first. The male shielded the young. He took two and did not fall. My archer loosed again. All three went down. The woman screamed." He paused. The word seemed to wound his mouth. "We moved to confirm the keep."

Polyonymous turned. The blue in her eyes had deepened until it was not a colour but a light.

"You," she said, and the word struck the air like a struck bell. "You were the shadow on the ridge."

Hymir held her gaze. "I wore a deer pin," he said. "It was my mark that winter."
Ragnar took a step toward his brother.

"Hymir."

"It was a clean action by the book," Hymir said quietly. "We did not know names. We did not know anything but positions and orders."

Polyonymous rose from the floor without bending her knees. The air lifted her the way fire lifts sparks. Her hair lifted as if in a current. Frost filmed across the walls in swift branching veins.

Ragnar lifted a hand. "Polyonymous."

Her voice came low and even. "I am done being small."

Lightning, blue as glacier light, braided through her irises. Hymir took an involuntary half step back. The torches along the corridor guttered as if a great breath had tried to blow them out.

Polyonymous lifted her palm. Thunder lived there. It cracked and leaped, not as a strike, but as a chain, a living rope of light that snapped around Hymir's arms and chest. He grunted as it locked him. He tried to move and could not.

Ragnar swore softly, half awe, half alarm. He reached her, but the air around her was charged and pushed against him like a tide.

"Listen to me," he said, voice steady by effort. "I am here. I am with you."

She looked from Hymir to Ragnar and back. Tears tracked clean lines down her face and steamed away before they reached her jaw. The room smelled suddenly of snow before a storm.

Hymir strained once, found no give, and

stilled. "If this is justice, take it," he said, and he meant it. "I have stood on enough ridges to know what I have bought."

The chain brightened. Ragnar flinched, then tried humor like a rope thrown across a chasm.

"Beloved," he said, breathless, "if you are going to do anything dramatic, perhaps wait until after I compliment your aim."

Her mouth flickered, almost a smile, then broke again. "He killed my family, my children."

Ragnar's voice roughened. "He killed strangers and made them his enemy because he did not know their names. He is not innocent. He is not your only answer."

Hymir forced his eyes to Ragnar. "You are

going to let her do this," he asked, hoarse.

"In all fairness," Ragnar said, chest heaving where a second bolt of light had wrapped his waist to keep him from intervening, "she did tell you last night she was going to take your kingdom. Who knew it would be today."

Even now, Hymir huffed a thin sound that might have been a laugh. "You jest like a man about to be struck by lightning."

"I jest like a man married to it," Ragnar said.

Polyonymous rose higher, until her braids brushed the ceiling. Snow sifted from the rafters. She looked down upon Hymir like a verdict.

"You want your life," she said. "Then you will give me the thing you value next to it. Your

crown. Your command. Your banners and your
men. Your roads and your stores. Your oath to
serve me and the living who cannot defend
themselves. The frost lands will not belong to
hands that treat mothers as sentinels."

Hymir stared up at her, face lit blue. For a long
breath he said nothing. Then something in his
shoulders lowered. He bowed as far as the
thunder would allow.

"My Queen," he said. The words shook the air.
"It is yours. I will hold what you ask me to
hold, and I will follow where you point."

The chains of lightning loosened.
Polyonymous floated down as if the anger had
been the only wind. Her boots touched the
floor. The last echo of thunder crawled along
the ice and faded.
She stood there trembling. Ragnar stepped to

her and folded her into his arms with a care that made his hands gentle despite his size.

"Breathe with me," he whispered. "In, and out."

Hymir straightened, raw but alive. He pressed a fist to his chest and bowed. "My Queen." He backed toward the door. "I will make the proclamation before noon." He hesitated. "For what it is worth, I am sorry."

Polyonymous did not answer. Hymir left.

They stood in the long hall. The ice around them held strange echoes. Polyonymous leaned her forehead between Ragnar's collarbones and let her breath find the rhythm of his. After a time, the lightning left her eyes, and the air in the hall remembered how to be still.

Ragnar brushed hair from her cheek. "I think,"
he said carefully, "that we should go home. We
can summon people who know more about
roads between worlds. We can ask why your
dreams carry weight. We can plan tomorrow
when your hands do not shake."

"By Odin's balls," he added under his breath,
half to himself, "I would prefer not to be
strung up by the waist again."

A laugh surprised her, wet and small, but real.
"Perhaps do not stand between me and a
thunderbolt next time."

"I will try to remember that" he said.
"Although I suspect I will fail, since I am an
idiot when it comes to you."

She drew back enough to meet his eyes. "I took
his crown."

"You took responsibility," Ragnar said. "There is a difference. One day you will choose if you want to wear it."

They walked out together. On the threshold she paused and looked back down the corridor where the wall had shown her a moment of her life like a candle in ice. She pressed her palm there. The surface was cold and smooth.

"Jötunn," she whispered. "Thiassi. Snoer. Snæbjörn. I will not forget you."

The ice said nothing. Outside, ravens lifted as they emerged, black marks against a white page. The sky had chosen blue again. Somewhere deep in the keep a bell began to ring to gather the lords for council, but whatever plan Hymir had meant to lay out at dawn would now be spoken in a different voice.

Ragnar helped her to the saddle. She squared her shoulders and set her hands on the reins.

"Home," he said.

"For now," she answered, and the words felt like a bridge that would hold them until they found a stronger one. They turned their horses toward the road and rode into the thin winter light, the new claim on a kingdom riding quietly between them.

Chapter 16, The Thunder at Home

The castle loomed above them, spires catching the faint light of dusk, banners stirring in the high winds as if whispering a welcome. Polyonymous and Ragnar rode beneath the gates, the iron portcullis lifting with a groan that echoed through the valley. Servants hurried into the courtyard, heads bowed, smiles breaking through their practiced composure at the sight of their lord and lady returned.

"My lord, my lady," the steward said, bending low, "new chambers have been made ready for you in the east wing, overlooking the valley. Until the south wing is restored and the ocean windows opened once more, you shall have the highest view of the frost plains."

Polyonymous inclined her head. Ragnar clapped the man on the shoulder. "East, west, or north," Ragnar boomed, "so long as it has a hearth and wine, it will do."

Before the steward could answer, a bellow split the air. Dreki. The young dragon came bounding down the inner steps, wings half-open, tail thrashing like a whip. His claws scrabbled on the flagstones, but his focus was only Ragnar.

"Dreki, you beast" Ragnar started, but too late. The dragon leapt, colliding with him full-force. Ragnar went sprawling to the stones, breath driven out of him, as Dreki stood over him, tongue lolling, drool spilling in thick strings across his beard.

Ragnar laughed even as he wrestled against the weight. "By Odin's hairy balls, Demi must have been feeding you thrice a day! You've grown again!"

The servants looked horrified, half-prepared to draw weapons, but Polyonymous only pressed her fingers to her lips to hide a smile.

"Off, you slobbering whelp," Ragnar gasped, wiping his face. "You'll drown me before any battle does."

The dragon barked a sound that was half roar, half puppy-yelp.

Ragnar sat up, wiping drool from his cheek, and raised his voice: "A feast! I am hungry enough to eat a dragon!"

The servants froze. Dreki's head snapped toward Ragnar, golden eyes wide. Polyonymous laughed aloud, the sound echoing across the courtyard. Ragnar lifted both hands, palms out. "No, no, little beast, peace! It was jest, only jest. You are safe from my belly."

Dreki snorted, huffed smoke, and nudged Ragnar's chest with a damp nose before retreating reluctantly.

The steward bowed again. "At once, my lord. The feast shall be laid."

Another servant stepped forward, bowing to Polyonymous. "And for you, my lady? What shall we prepare?"

Polyonymous exhaled wearily. "Draw me a bath," she said. "Let me wash the road from my skin."

The east wing chambers glowed with firelight, steam curling from the copper tub set near the hearth. The maidens bowed and reached for soaps and oils, but Ragnar's hand swept them gently toward the door.

"Out," he said. "I will see to my wife."

Polyonymous raised one brow but did not object as Ragnar disrobed, the scars of old battles stark in the glow. He stepped into the water behind her, hands broad and tender as he drew the cloth across her shoulders.

"You wield lightning now," Ragnar murmured, trailing a kiss along her neck. "Thunder in your hands, storms in your eyes. A man might think twice before teasing you again."

She leaned forward, silent.

He continued softly, lips brushing her ear:

"These dreams these lives you walk through they feel real to you. But remember this, my love. Two years ago, you stood before the gods with me. You were wed to me. Whatever you see in frost or fire, it cannot be you, for you are mine."

Polyonymous stiffened. She pulled from his hands, rising from the bath, water streaming from her skin like silver threads. "Do not speak of them as shadows," she said. "They were real. More real than I can bear."

"My love" Ragnar began, reaching.

"I want to lie down," she said, wrapping a robe around her shoulders. "I am not hungry."

"Polyonymous"

"Later," she cut him off, and left the chamber

with wet footprints fading into the hall.

The east chamber windows framed the valley, a sweep of silver fields beneath a rising moon. Polyonymous sat on the edge of the bed, her hands in her lap. Each finger tapped her thumb in slow rhythm. Tiny sparks crackled between them, little bolts of blue-white lightning leaping from fingertip to fingertip. Her eyes glowed faintly, an eerie, steady light.

The door opened. Ragnar entered with two servants, one bearing wine, the other a tray of roasted meats and bread. He stopped at the threshold, his gaze caught by her glowing eyes, the sparks dancing in her hands.

"My love," he said carefully, voice low. "I have brought food. And wine."

Neither her head nor her eyes turned. The sparks continued to jump, sharp little zaps that stung the air.

The servants froze. Ragnar lifted a hand, motioning them back. "Leave us," he said quietly. They hesitated, then began to turn.

A thunderous crash shook the door wide. Dreki barrelled into the chamber, tongue lolling, joy uncontainable. "No!" Ragnar roared, throwing himself aside. "Not now!"

But Dreki leapt anyway, paws landing on the bed, the mattress collapsing under his weight. He slobbered over Polyonymous's face, licking and nudging, tail thudding against the wall.

A sound broke the air Polyonymous laughing, the glow fading from her eyes. "Dreki! You little beast you never let me rest."

She pushed his snout away gently, chuckling even as his drool soaked her robe.

Ragnar, half-buried under an overturned tray of bread, gave a shaky laugh. "By the gods, I thought his days were numbered down to seconds. But no, it seems he alone can survive your storms."

Polyonymous stroked Dreki's muzzle. Her hands no longer sparked, only trembled faintly.

Ragnar pushed himself upright, brushing crumbs from his tunic. "You are changing," he said, voice softer now, the humor fading into something more solemn. "By the gods, it is no jest. I think they have a hand in this. I swear on Odin himself, we will find the truth." Polyonymous leaned her forehead against Dreki's brow, whispering something Ragnar could not hear. The dragon hummed low in his chest, content.

153

And outside the window, thunder muttered in a sky that had been clear.

Chapter 17, Steel, Sobs, and Smoke

The clang of iron rang across the training yard. Sparks leapt like startled fireflies every time Ragnar's blade met Bjorn's. The ground was scarred from a hundred past duels, yet it never tired of their footsteps.

"Again!" Ragnar barked, chest heaving, sweat streaking down his arms.

Bjorn, older, broader, and smug as a cat in cream, rolled his shoulders. "If I keep beating you like this, my lord, your men will start calling me king."

"Keep talking, chef," Ragnar growled, swinging a heavy arc meant to shut him up.

The steel met, echoed, and slid.

"You've been brooding again," Bjorn said between blows, eyes narrowed. "The queen's dreams?"

Ragnar's guard faltered for a blink. "She is with them," he muttered, striking harder. "Other kings. Other worlds. She smiles, she touches, she" His sword caught with a snarl of sparks. "It's just a dream," he said louder, almost to himself. "Just a dream, Ragnar, you fool."

Bjorn shoved him back with a flat strike to the chest that sent Ragnar stumbling into the dirt. "Dream or not, you look like a puppy left outside in the rain. Man up."

Ragnar sat there, sword across his knees, eyes shining. "But Bjorn, she laughed. She laughed with him the way she laughs with me." His voice cracked. He sniffed. "Do you know how that feels?"

Bjorn planted the sword in the ground, leaning on it like a farmer on a spade. "Like getting slapped by Odin and kissed by Loki, all in the same breath."

Ragnar nodded miserably. "Exactly." He wiped his nose with the back of his arm. "It's not cheating if it's a dream, right?"

Bjorn smirked. "Not unless you're losing the dream-battle to another king. Then maybe."

Ragnar's bottom lip trembled. Then, with a sudden roar, he sprang to his feet, wiping away tears with the ferocity of a storm. "No more! I am Ragnar, breaker of shields, king of the hill!" He lunged, swinging his blade in a blaze of sparks.

Bjorn laughed as the swords clashed again, this time with Ragnar fighting like a man who had sobbed all the water out of his body and was determined to refill it with glory.

"Better," Bjorn grunted, parrying blow after blow. "Now you're fighting like a man who wants his wife to stop laughing in dreams."

"By Odin's balls, I'll make her laugh only at me!" Ragnar bellowed.

The men cheered from the sidelines.

Then Dreki bounded into the yard.

The dragon pup barrelled between them, tail swinging like a wrecking ball. His massive hindquarters smacked into the smith's fire. The coals scattered, rolling across the ground like angry stars.

"Dreki!" Ragnar shouted, leaping aside as a stray ember caught the edge of his cape. Smoke curled upward. "Not the cape! This is bear hide!"

Dreki yipped happily, unaware, tail sweeping through a rack of training spears. They clattered like wind chimes of doom.

"Fire!" someone screamed.

A flower stand toppled, petals raining down into the fire. For a moment, it looked like a wedding pyre for buttercups. Then the flames licked the curtain of a nearby villager's hut.

"Put it out!"

Ragnar, cape smoking, stomped the flames with his boot. Bjorn casually grabbed a bucket and dumped it over the hut, water sloshing everywhere. The villagers wailed.

"Relax," Bjorn said dryly. "We've put out worse."

"Worse?!" the smith shouted, waving at his scattered coals.

Ragnar ripped off the smouldering cape and threw it over the curtain, smothering the fire, while Dreki pounced on a barrel of apples, smashing it to splinters. Apples rolled across the yard like tiny cannonballs. Soldiers slipped, curses flying.

Through it all, Ragnar and Bjorn barely broke stride in their duel, still trading blows even as they stomped out fires in between swings.

"You call this chaos?" Ragnar yelled, laughing madly. "This is Tuesday!"

Bjorn's sword clanged against his. "Then by the gods, I dread to see Wednesday."

Dreki bounded back, proudly carrying half of Ragnar's singed cape in his jaws like a prize. Ragnar doubled over, wheezing with laughter, sword still in hand.

And for a moment, amid fire, smoke, and sobs, the training yard was alive with the ridiculousness of men, dragons, and dreams that felt too real.

Interlude 7 – The Fire King

The cool evening breeze of Midgard lulled Polyonymous as she lay beside Ragnar, his hand resting heavy and protective across her waist. She pressed a goodnight kiss to his cheek, his breathing already beginning to even out into sleep. Her own eyes grew heavy, the distant songs of the night settling into silence.

But as she drifted deeper, warmth replaced the cool air. The comfort of the sheets melted into waves of heat, pulsing like the heart of a forge. Sweat prickled at her brow. The warmth turned into fire, too hot, too consuming. She gasped and opened her eyes.

The world around her burned.

She was no longer in Midgard, no longer in her

chamber with Ragnar. She stood in the middle of a battlefield where flame roared like thunder. Fire giants towered over her, their molten skin cracking with veins of lava, swords the size of trees clashing in titanic arcs. Mythical beasts, their hides of ember and ash, lunged at one another with savage fury. The air shimmered with heat, sparks raining down like deadly snow.

Polyonymous stumbled back, shielding her face. Her skin glowed faintly, her arms lit with a strange flame that did not burn. It shimmered over her like a cloak, licking harmlessly along her body. Confusion rattled her.

"Polyonymous!"

The voice boomed over the battlefield, deep as a mountain breaking. She turned just as a massive shadow swooped across the firelit ground. From the smoke emerged a warrior of flame incarnate, every stride splitting the ground beneath him. His body radiated with heat, hair burning upward like a living inferno, and his eyes glowed molten gold.

With a thundering roar, he flung her a sword, its blade shimmering with fire runes. "Get behind me!"

She caught it by instinct, the heat searing her palm, but no pain followed. The blade belonged in her hand as though it had always been there.

The warrior tore through the giants with brutal swiftness, his massive blade cleaving molten flesh. Sparks and embers exploded in his wake as he planted himself before her, towering, unyielding. "What in the gods' name are you doing on a battlefield?" he barked.

"I, I don't know," she stammered, the firelight painting her face. Her voice trembled. "Who… who are you?"

His brows shot upward, disbelief etched across his molten features. "Who am I?" He leaned in close, his fire dimming just enough to reveal the face of a man, impossibly handsome, his skin bronze and perfect, his hair falling black and shimmering like obsidian when not aflame. "Surely you recognize your own husband… your king."

Her lips parted in shock. She shook her head faintly. "Please, tell me your name."

He smirked, though there was pain in his gaze. "Surtr." His voice cracked like firewood snapping. He gave a low laugh, pulling her against him. "You've lost your memory, then.

A blow to the head, no doubt. No matter. We'll have the healers look at you."

She blinked up at him, the heat of his embrace not scalding, but warm, like the sun's core. His arm around her was protective, fierce. Her confusion deepened.

The battle raged on in the distance, but she was carried swiftly from it, Surtr refusing to let her feet stumble. The healers came, beings made of ember and ash, with eyes glowing like coal. They gave her a draught, thick, smoky, and sweet, that pulled her down into slumber.

When she woke again, the fire had dimmed, the sounds of war replaced with silence. She was in a chamber carved of blackened stone, glowing rivers of magma tracing through the walls like veins of fire. She sat up slowly, the air warm and heavy.

Surtr was there, waiting at her bedside. His flames were gone now, replaced by the form of a man tall, broad, his shoulders draped in obsidian-black armour. His eyes still burned faintly, and when he smiled, it was devastating.

"That must have been some blow to your head," he said, voice softer now, though still edged with thunder. "Do you remember nothing? Not how you came to be on that battlefield? It is no place for my queen."

"My… queen?" she whispered.

He cupped her face gently, thumb brushing her cheek with surprising tenderness. "Aye. My queen. My Polyonymous." His voice was a vow. "You belong here. With me."

Her lips parted, a soft, uncertain smile breaking through the haze. His warmth washed over her, and for a heartbeat she allowed herself to lean into him.

He bent, pulling her into his arms. His lips hovered close, the fire in his eyes dimming into something almost human, almost vulnerable.

And then…

Her eyes opened to the cool darkness of Midgard. Ragnar lay beside her, breathing steady, the night breeze once again cool and gentle. She sat up, clutching the sheets, her heart racing.

The memory of the flames lingered. The fire on her skin. The warmth of Surtr's embrace.

She touched her lips, trembling.

It felt real. Too real. And yet, distant, as though slipping through her fingers like smoke.

She looked at Ragnar, sleeping peacefully. Was this the dream? Or was the fire realm the dream?

She lay back, confusion heavy as stone on her chest. For the first time, she feared closing her eyes.

Chapter 18 – The Council and the Forgotten Past

The horns sounded at dawn, echoing across the valley. From the east wing balcony, Polyonymous stood with Ragnar, watching as the council's procession wound its way up the mountain path. Banners of gold and silver shimmered in the morning light, and the voices of heralds rose in chants that spoke of lineage, law, and duty.

The gates swung open, and the riders entered, cloaks dusted with the road, but their presence regal, nonetheless. Servants hurried to greet them, and Ragnar himself strode forward, cloak sweeping the ground, his voice booming.

"Welcome, councillors! Our hearth is yours;

our tables are yours, and tonight, our wine will flow until you forget the burden of travel."

Laughter followed, but the air quickly settled into solemnity as the council assembled in the grand hall.

The fire crackled in the great hearth, casting shadows long as memory. The council's leader, an elder with silver hair braided to his waist, rose to speak. His voice was low but carried across the chamber.

"We come with answers," he said. "Or as many as we have the strength to give. You were given a child. A babe, wrapped in furs and left in our care with the mark of destiny carved unseen upon her. We were told to raise her as our own, and so we did."

Polyonymous's breath caught, her fingers curling around the carved armrest of her chair. Ragnar's eyes narrowed, sharp as steel.

The elder continued. "When she came of age, we sent her to the monastery, where young princesses learn the crafts of queenship letters, governance, the lore of the old gods. When her education was complete, she returned, as was foretold. From there, she was trained in the arts of battle, and she became the warrior you see now fearless, unyielding."

Polyonymous whispered, "But my powers? The storms, the lightning no one told you of them?"

The councillors exchanged uneasy glances. The elder spread his hands. "No, my queen. Of these powers we were never told. They were not part of the charge we were given. If such truths exist, they were kept from us as well."

Ragnar leaned forward, his voice thundering across the table. "Then tell us this who gave you the child. Who were her true blood? Where might we find them?"

Silence filled the hall. The elder shook his head; sorrow etched into the lines of his face. "We do not know. We were not told. We were only entrusted with the child and warned that questions of blood might one day cost lives."

Ragnar slammed his hand on the table, the dishes rattling. "By Odin's hammer, you speak of shadows and half-truths! A daughter is not a mystery to be handed down like coin."

Polyonymous touched his arm, steadying him. Her eyes were glassy, though her voice was steady. "If they do not know, then we press no further today. The truth will come to light in its time."

That evening, the great hall was transformed. Tables groaned under the weight of roasted boar, steaming breads, honeyed fruits, and wine flowing like rivers. Musicians played harps and horns, dancers whirled in silks the colour of flame, and even Dreki was bribed into calmness with a barrel of smoked meat set just outside the hall.

Councillors laughed and feasted, grateful for the respite. Stories of battles and victories filled the air, though always the unspoken weight of what had been revealed hung in the shadows.

When the last toast was raised and the final song sung, Ragnar rose, lifting his goblet. His voice carried through the rafters.

"Tonight you are under our roof, safe and welcome. Tomorrow, you ride and may the road be kind to you. But remember this whatever her blood, whatever her destiny, she is my queen. She is ours. And the world will know her name."

The hall erupted in cheers, the councillors raising their cups high. Polyonymous sat at Ragnar's side, heart heavy and light all at once, her fingers curling against his.

For though her past had been hidden, her present burned bright. And her future like a storm on the horizon was still to come.

Chapter 19 – Dreki and the Egg of Pearls

The morning mist clung low to the forest floor, and Ragnar whistled as he trudged along the game trail, cloak swinging at his heels. Beside him bounded Dreki, the dragon pup nearly as tall as a horse now, wings clumsy, tail swishing like a battering ram.

"Come then, little beast," Ragnar chuckled, patting the side of his leg as if Dreki were some oversized hounds. "Let us see what mischief the gods have laid for us today."

The forest answered with birdsong and rustling leaves. Dreki's nose pressed eagerly to the ground, and before long, the dragon lunged headlong into a thicket. A squeal split the air, a rabbit bolted out, fur a blur of white.

"Catch it, Dreki!" Ragnar roared, clapping his hands like a madman.

Dreki pounced. He missed spectacularly. His hind legs tangled in roots, wings flared at the wrong moment, and he toppled forward, somersaulting nose-first into the mud. His tail stuck straight up like a flagpole, and the rabbit darted away, fluffy tail twitching.

Ragnar dropped to his knees, howling with laughter. "By Odin's balls, you're as graceful as a one-eyed goat on ice!" He wiped tears from his eyes as Dreki huffed indignantly, mud dripping from his snout.

The morning continued no better for Dreki. At the riverbank, he plunged after silver fish, snapping his jaws at the ripples. Each time he came up sputtering, with nothing but weeds dangling from his teeth. Once, he leapt so high he landed belly-first in the water with a splash that sent Ragnar reeling onto his back in hysterics.

"You'll starve us both, little one," Ragnar wheezed, clutching his ribs. "If Polyonymous hears of this, she'll make me take up fishing instead!"

By midday, man and dragon were muddy, wet, and laughing still. It was then that Dreki froze, nose twitching. He padded slowly toward the ruins of an old stone wall, half-swallowed by ivy and moss. Ragnar followed, brushing aside vines.

There, in a shallow nest of stone and earth, lay an egg. Large as a shield, its surface cracked with age, dulled to a grey sheen.

Dreki nudged it gently with his snout, chirping

low.

Ragnar crouched, frowning. "Sorry, little beast. Too old. The spark's gone. It will never hatch." He laid a hand on Dreki's neck. "We should go."

But Dreki refused. With a stubborn huff, he opened his jaws and exhaled a gout of flame over the egg. Fire licked across its surface, smoke rising in lazy curls.

Ragnar waved a hand, coughing. "By Odin's hairy balls, what are you doing? If you think you're eating it, don't! After all these years, it'd taste of nothing but ash and disappointment."

And then…

The egg moved.
Ragnar stopped mid-laugh, blinking. A crack

spread across the shell, glowing faintly from within. Another crack. Then another. The sound of splitting stone filled the glade.

With a final shudder, the egg broke apart, and from the shards emerged a dragon no larger than a hunting dog. Its scales shimmered like pearl, white and opalescent, reflecting the sunlight in hues of blue and gold. Enormous eyes blinked up at Ragnarliquid, innocent, and filled with wonder.

Dreki froze, tail stiff, wings tucked. For the first time in his life, he was utterly silent. The baby dragon squeaked softly, tilting its head at him.

Ragnar glanced between them, his jaw slack. Then, slowly, the corners of his mouth curled into a grin. "Well," he said, voice hushed, "I suppose the gods weren't finished with you after all."

The pearl-scaled hatchling tumbled forward, bumping into Dreki's chest. Dreki snorted, then lowered his head and gave the little one a sloppy lick, earning a squeal of delight.

Ragnar threw back his head and laughed. "By Odin's balls, Polyonymous will have my hide if I return with another dragon, but damn it, you're coming with us. A finer gift for my queen I cannot imagine."

He ruffled Dreki's neck ridges, still chuckling. "Looks like you've got yourself a sister now, little beast. And perhaps she'll even manage to catch a rabbit better than you do."

Dreki grumbled but pressed closer to the hatchling, curling protectively around her as if already claiming her as kin. Ragnar sighed, wiping mud from his boots, and shook his head in disbelief.

Two dragons. What could possibly go wrong?

Chapter 20 – The Naming of Máni

The great hall was alive with firelight when Ragnar entered, mud still clinging to his boots. Over his shoulder, Dreki waddled proudly, tail high, wings clumsy as ever. Cradled against Ragnar's chest, wrapped in his cloak, was the pearl-scaled hatchling, blinking up at the vaulted ceiling with wide, curious eyes.

Polyonymous looked up from her seat at the long table, brows lifting. "By Odin's balls, Ragnar," she exclaimed, rising. "You've brought home *another* dragon?"

Ragnar grinned sheepishly, setting the little creature on the table. "Before you scold me, my love, let me say this one was Dreki's doing."

Dreki thumped his tail against the floor, eyes fixed proudly on the hatchling as if to say, *Yes, this is my idea and my prize.*

The baby dragon squeaked and wobbled toward Polyonymous, its scales shimmering with hues of white, silver, and faint blue, like moonlight on snow. Polyonymous' expression softened at once. She held out her hands and the hatchling leapt clumsily into her arms, curling against her chest with a purr like crackling embers.

"Oh, Ragnar," she whispered, stroking the smooth pearl scales. "She's beautiful."

Ragnar chuckled, scratching his beard. "Beautiful trouble, more like. By Odin's hairy balls, she'll turn this place upside down before long."

Polyonymous ignored him, eyes shining. "Her name is Máni."

At the sound of her new name, the dragonlet squeaked again, eyes glowing faintly. Dreki bounded forward and nudged her with his snout, almost knocking her from Polyonymous' arms.

"Careful, Dreki!" Ragnar barked, though he was laughing. "You'll smother your sister before she's even learned to breathe fire."

Weeks passed, and the castle soon learned that one dragon pup was chaos but two were utter mayhem.

Máni grew quickly, her wings strong enough to glide down the halls, while Dreki's clumsy bulk thundered after her. Together they tore through corridors like living storms, scattering servants and sending tapestries swaying from the walls.

One evening, Ragnar and Polyonymous sat in the hall when a crash echoed above them. They looked up just in time to see Máni and Dreki tumble down the staircase in a heap of wings, claws, and squeals. They landed in a burst of broken rushes, Dreki's tail tangled in a curtain, Máni proudly perched atop his belly like a conquering queen.

"By Odin's balls," Ragnar groaned, covering his face with both hands. "First they'll bring the roof down, then the whole bloody kingdom."

Polyonymous only laughed, tears springing to her eyes. "They're children. Let them play." "Play?" Ragnar exclaimed, pointing as a servant ran past shrieking, chased by both dragons with tongues lolling happily. "That's not play, that's a siege!"

Polyonymous smirked, leaning back in her chair. "A siege with very sharp teeth."

Máni scampered up onto the table, scattering bread and fruit, before leaping to Polyonymous' lap. Dreki attempted to follow but crashed halfway through, his hindquarters swinging and sending a goblet of wine flying straight into Ragnar's lap.

Ragnar shot to his feet, dripping, and roared, "By Odin's balls, Dreki!"

Polyonymous burst into helpless laughter, clutching Máni as she wriggled and purred. "See?" she said between giggles. "They're a gift."

Ragnar glowered at his soaked tunic, then at his wife's bright eyes. At last, he sighed, sinking back into his chair with a reluctant grin. "A gift from the gods, or a curse from Loki. Either way, we're doomed."

The two dragons bounded off again, tails knocking goblets and candlesticks to the floor, while their laughter rang through the hall queen, king, and dragons together in their chaos.

Chapter 21: The Seaside Lessons

The sea was her cathedral.

Every morning and every dusk, when Ragnar took the dragons across the castle ruins and hillside to stretch their wings and tumble through broken arches, Polyonymous sought the rocky shore.

There, with waves gnawing the black stone and gulls crying overhead, she spread her notes, herbs, and bottles across driftwood and tide-worn boulders. Candles guttered stubbornly in the sea breeze, their flames dancing like restless spirits. Scrolls, smudged with saltwater and ink, sprawled open at her bare feet.

Her silver hair, braided in long coils, slipped over her shoulders as she ground herbs into a paste.

"Völva and læknir," she whispered, almost as if testing the words on her tongue. Seer and healer. Threads of the unseen and salves of the earth. These disciplines drew her like a tide she could not resist.

The sea answered with its steady thunder.

The Lightning Within

That evening, the clouds swelled like dark sails above the cliffs. Polyonymous lifted her hand, letting a filament of lightning crawl across her fingertips. It obeyed her now.

Not the reckless storms of her rage, not the uncontrolled bursts that had once left her trembling this was precision. A silver thread she could weave, shape, and return to the sky.

She extended her arm, and the bolt leapt, striking the air above the waves with a crack that echoed across the cliffs. She laughed, a clear, surprised laugh that startled the gulls into flight.

"Better," she murmured, closing her fist as the spark recoiled into her palm like a trained hawk. "Not anger… not grief. Just will."

A voice carried over the stones.

"You're frightening the fish again."

Ragnar approached with a grin, boots crunching on gravel. Dreki and little Máni bounded behind him, tails lashing, wings half-unfurled.

"They'll swim deeper if you keep calling down the heavens like that," he teased, though his

eyes lingered on her hands with awe. "One day you'll burn my beard clean off."

She smirked, lowering her hands. "If your beard survives the dragons' antics, it will survive me."

Ragnar threw back his head and laughed, ruffling Dreki's scales as the dragonlet tried to climb his leg.

The Healer's Path

By daylight, her work was quieter. She bent over jars of seawater tinctures, mixing kelp and powdered shells with mountain herbs Ragnar's men brought from their hunts. Some healed fever, some eased wounds, and others she suspected could kill as easily as they cured.

She spoke to herself as she worked, whispering the names of plants and bones, cataloguing them like an apprentice.

"Læknir," she said softly, touching a salve to her wrist where an old scar burned faintly. "I will not only strike. I will mend."

Her candlelight study hours stretched longer and longer. Sometimes Ragnar found her asleep among her scrolls, ink staining her fingertips, a dragon curled protectively at her feet.

Between Duty and Calling

"You vanish, little queen," Ragnar chided her one night as they sat by the shore, stars glinting in the black tide. His tone was playful, but beneath it was a thread of concern.

Polyonymous tore her gaze from the constellation of moons above. "I... lose time," she admitted. "Every herb I crush, every rune I trace it feels like I am drawing closer to the gods. Closer to answers."

"And further from your duties."

She frowned, then caught the mischief in his eye. "You mock me."

"Only a little," Ragnar said with a chuckle. "But if the throne hall grows dusty, the people will mutter that their queen is hiding with bottles and bones instead of leading them."

Her lips curved, though guilt tugged at her chest. "And if I do not learn this, Ragnar? If I cannot master the sight, the storm, and the healing what kind of queen will I be then?"

Ragnar leaned closer, brushing a salt-tangled strand of her hair from her cheek. "The kind who terrifies her enemies and heals her people. The kind the gods themselves will think twice before crossing."

His words sank deep, steadying her. She smiled faintly, then pressed her palm to his. The lightning hummed there, quiet and controlled, dancing like a secret between their joined hands.

The Seer's Quiet

That night, she dreamt only shadows. A hall of mirrors, each pane holding a different future, some glorious, some terrible. Her reflection whispered in voices not her own.

She woke breathless, the taste of prophecy sharp on her tongue.

The sea hissed at her feet. The dragons stirred restlessly. Ragnar's laughter echoed faintly from the ruins above.

Polyonymous exhaled, straightened her shoulders, and lit another candle.

The gods would not wait. And neither would she.

Chapter 22: The Healer's Vow

The sea whispered as always, but tonight Polyonymous' calm practice was interrupted by the thunder of hooves. Ragnar's cousin Leif rode hard across the cliffs, his silver hair tangled, his fine robe dusted with dirt and sweat. In his arms he cradled a small bundle, a child, pale and fevered. Behind him trailed two guards carrying another, younger babe wrapped in dark cloth, little Rollo, whose wide eyes blinked at the night as if he sensed the storm in the air.

Leif's voice cracked before he even dismounted.

"Polyonymous, for the love of the gods, help us, my daughter will not wake. The fever will take her." He slid from the saddle and almost fell, then stumbled forward with the child. The horses stamped and tossed their heads as if they also felt the urgency, and the salty wind snatched Leif's words and threw them against the rocks.

Ragnar rushed forward, startled, but it was Polyonymous who rose at once, her skirts sweeping the stones. Her eyes went to the girl, the little princess whose lips were too pale and whose breaths came too shallow. She did not hesitate.

"Give her to me," she said, her voice steady with the calm that entered her whenever a life hung in the balance.
Leif surrendered the child as though handing over his own heart. His hands shook; his eyes shone with desperation. "I tried the healers in the mountain towns," he said, "but the fever only climbed. She speaks in her sleep, and her

eyes do not see me. If she dies, I will have nothing left but Rollo."

Polyonymous laid the girl on a blanket beside the driftwood table that served as her shore side workbench. Candles bracketed the edges like watchful sentries. Around them, bowls of seawater, ground herbs, pieces of driftwood, and vials of potion waited. Ragnar knelt at her side, uncertain but present, while Leif hovered, fists clenched, his baby Rollo cradled in his other arm.

"What is her name," Polyonymous asked, bending close to the child's face. She felt the breath, thin as a thread, warm against her cheek. She placed her palm against the girl's forehead and closed her eyes.

"Sigrid," Leif replied. "She is my bright victory, or she was, before this shadow took her."

Polyonymous opened her satchel and measured pinches of powdered kelp, willow bark, and crushed salt crystals. She added them to a shallow bowl and poured in seawater until the mixture turned a faint blue. "She burns inside and yet her skin is cold," she murmured. "This is no simple fever. There is damp in the lungs, and something that clings to the spirit."

Leif flinched. "Cursed, then," he whispered.

"No," Polyonymous said, her tone firm. "Poisoned by the world itself. Marsh air, Mold, grief that has not been spoken, all of it can tangle. I will draw it out."

She dipped two fingers into the bowl and traced runes along the child's collarbone and down to the sternum. The marks shone for a moment, then faded into the skin. As she worked, her fingertips began to hum. Lightning woke in the small bones of her hands, obedient to intention, not to rage. The spark rode her knuckles like a tame foxfire and leaped from mark to mark. Ragnar's breath caught, and Leif took an involuntary step back.

"Wife," Ragnar said quietly, "is this safe." Polyonymous did not look up. "Do you doubt me, Ragnar."

He tried to smile and failed. "Only when your hands mimic Thor in a bad mood."

"Then stand close and be still," she said, and the corner of her mouth twitched. "And if you must pray, do it under your breath."

She placed one hand at Sigrid's throat and the other over the tiny rib cage. The storm in her blood changed pitch. It was music, gentle and steady, the kind a mother hums without knowing it. Lightning did not strike the sky. It threaded inward, a silver current that warmed the child from the inside out.

The little chest spasmed. A wet cough rattled the silence. Sticky phlegm bubbled at the girl's lips. Ragnar leaned in with a cloth and wiped it away while Leif choked on a sob.

Sigrid's eyes fluttered and rolled, then stilled again.

Her breath came a little deeper. Polyonymous exhaled and reached for a clay bottle. "This is sea thyme, boiled with winter honey and a scrap of iron," she said. "It brings back those who wander too far from their bodies. A drop will be enough."

She tipped a single drop onto Sigrid's tongue. The girl swallowed reflexively. A moment later her fingers twitched. A small sound, almost a word, slipped out. Leif dropped to his knees, clutching Rollo tighter. "By the Allfather," he whispered.

"You have found her."

Polyonymous kept her hands on the child, anchoring the breath. "We are not done," she said softly. "The fever will fight us." She looked up at Leif. "When did this begin."

Leif dragged a hand over his face. "Three nights ago," he said. "She was playing by the riverbank in the marsh valley. I was foolish. I wanted to show her the silver reeds that sing when the wind comes from the east. She slipped, only for a moment, and swallowed water."

"Marsh water holds old things," Polyonymous said.

"Not all of them want to leave." She frowned, feeling along Sigrid's ribs. "She needs warmth, but not too much, and she needs air that moves. Ragnar, build us a wind path from the door to the fire pit.

Leif, lay Rollo on the blanket by you and wash your hands with salt water. You will help me grind the fennel seeds."

Ragnar moved as told, pulling the driftwood table aside, arranging stones to coax a corridor for the sea breeze. Leif obeyed with the focus of a soldier, his fear disciplined by the tasks.

When he returned, Polyonymous placed a
mortar between them.

Together they ground the seeds and added
dried lungwort and a ribbon of seal fat that
had been rendered the day before. The air
filled with a clean, bracing scent.

While they worked, Rollo began to fuss, his
tiny face folding. Ragnar scooped him up
without thinking. The large man swayed as if
he had done this all his life, which he had not,
and hummed a low, rumbling tune that
sounded suspiciously like a battle song played
at half speed. Rollo hiccupped, grabbed
Ragnar's beard, and promptly fell asleep.
Leif stared in astonishment, then gave a broken
laugh that turned to tears. "Thank you," he
said hoarsely.

"Hush," Ragnar replied, cradling the boy against his chest. "Your daughter is busy fighting, and your son is busy drooling. Both are excellent signs."

Polyonymous gathered the poultice they had made and pressed it to Sigrid's chest. She wrapped the child in a clean linen that had been warmed by the fire. Then she lifted her face to the open sky where the moons hung bright. "Hear me," she whispered, not loudly and not in panic, "she belongs to life, not to the places under the reeds. Give her back."

A faint roll of thunder answered from far out at sea.

Lightning threaded the clouds like a seamstress tucking a silver stitch through blue cloth. It was not the frenzy she had felt in other battles. It was companionship. The world agreed with her. The breeze shifted and entered the makeshift corridor Ragnar had built, then slipped across Sigrid's face.

The child's body relaxed, breath by breath. Night deepened. The waves kept time. Ragnar carried Rollo into the hall and returned with blankets and a proper pillow. Leif would not sit until Polyonymous seized his wrist and pressed him down on the pillow. "If you fall over, you are no help to either child," she said. "Drink this." She handed him a steaming cup filled with fennel tea and a swirl of honey. "You must breathe slowly and match the sound of the waves. Your daughter will follow you."

Leif obeyed. Slowly the tightness in his shoulders loosened. He watched Polyonymous tend Sigrid with the relentless gentleness of tidewater wearing away stone. At times the fever surged, and the girl tossed her head, whispering to things only she could see. At those moments Polyonymous steadied her with both hands and sang low, a song that had no words and yet understood every fear a child carries into sleep.

Near midnight the fever peaked. Heat poured off the small body like summer from a black rock. Ragnar set a bowl of cool seawater by Polyonymous and refreshed the cloths as fast as she could ask for them. Leif whispered prayers to every god he had ever met and several he had not. Rollo woke and cried, and Ragnar, faced with an enemy he could defeat, offered the boy his finger. Rollo gnawed it with fierce satisfaction and quieted again.

Polyonymous tried a second mixture, one meant to pull heat without stealing strength. She made it from crushed pearl, ground poppy heads, and a hint of bitter yarrow. She placed the bowl beneath Sigrid's nose and let the steam rise. "Breathe, little one," she coaxed. "Do not be afraid. The world is large, and it has room for you."

Sigrid's lashes fluttered. A tear formed at the corner of her eye and slid down into her hair. She swallowed and the pulse in her throat grew steadier.

When the next cough came, it was productive. A dark clot lifted from her lungs, and with it the reek of marsh decay. Leif made a strangled sound.

Polyonymous nodded. "There it is," she said. "The piece that would not let go. Now we must give her back her warmth."

They fed her small sips of broth. They changed the linens. They tucked warm stones at her feet. An hour later, Sigrid opened her eyes fully. They were glazed at first, then cleared, and she focused on the light above her. She turned her head toward the sound of the sea and then toward the sound of her father's breath. "Papa," she whispered.

Leif fell forward, his forehead against her small hand. He laughed and cried at once. "I am here, my star," he said. "I am here." He looked up at Polyonymous, shame and gratitude fighting in his face. "I should have kept her away from the marsh. I should have known better."

"You wanted to show her something beautiful," Polyonymous said. "Beauty always carries risk. You will teach her how to choose, that is all."

Sigrid slept again, this time naturally. Rollo slept as well, limp and warm against Ragnar's shoulder. The castle settled into a hush full of breathing and small pops from the fire. Polyonymous sat back on her heels. The world had not only given the child back, it had given something to Polyonymous as well, a certainty that her gift did not exist simply to strike or to defend. It existed to restore.

Leif insisted on carrying Sigrid into the great hall himself. Ragnar led the way, still rocking Rollo with an absent tenderness. In the hall, guards made space by the hearth. Old women who had come to stoke the fires muttered blessings. One pressed a woven charm into Polyonymous' palm. "A fisher's knot," the woman said. "For binding breath to bone."

For three days they stayed. Sigrid's strength returned slowly, then faster, as children often do.

She took broth from a cup, then chewed soft bread, then demanded a slice of pear and ate it with grave determination. Polyonymous took her into the courtyard each afternoon and taught her how to breathe like the sea, out longer than in, calm and steady. Ragnar carried Rollo around like a hairy and extremely proud ship mast, which allowed Leif to sleep for the first time in a week. Whenever Ragnar tried to give the boy back, Rollo clung to his beard in protest. "Traitor," Leif told his son with a tired smile, and Ragnar puffed with secret pleasure.

On the second night, a storm tried to climb ashore. The windows trembled, and the dragons beyond the wall answered the sky with their own rolling voices.

Ragnar moved to bar the shutters, but Polyonymous shook her head. "Let the air move," she said.

"Sigrid must learn to hear thunder without fear."

She sat with the child by the window and counted flashes. For each flash, Sigrid pressed her fingers into Polyonymous' palm and whispered the number.

By the tenth the fear drained from her shoulders. By the thirteenth she smiled at the sky.
Leif watched them with an expression Ragnar had never seen on his cousin, something like awe. When Polyonymous tucked Sigrid into bed, Leif approached her with his head bowed. "I brought coin," he said. "I will bring more. I

will bring anything you ask. Name a price and I will pay it."

Polyonymous shook her head. "There is no price," she said. "There is only a vow. While you are under our roof, your children are mine to protect as if they were my own. When you return home, you will teach others what you learned here. Keep clean water at the hearth. Air the rooms. Breathe with your children when they are afraid. When the world tangles around them, help them untie it."

Leif swallowed hard. He went to one knee and kissed her hand, a gesture he had never offered any queen. "Then I will carry your vow to my people," he said. "They will know your name as healer, and they will speak it with gratitude."

That night, while the storm passed on to trouble other shores, Polyonymous dreamed. She stood again on the rocks by the sea, only now the moons hung very low, and their light painted the waves with paths of milk. A figure stepped onto the nearest path, not a god she knew, but a woman with seaweed caught in her hair and eyes like tide pools.

The woman touched Polyonymous' hands. "You ask only to return what was taken," she said. "This is good. But remember, healer, that sometimes the world takes because it must change shape. When you feel that pull, do not fight it, guide it."
Polyonymous woke before dawn, the dream humming in her fingers. She went to the window.

The storm had left the air clean and precise. Ragnar appeared beside her, barefoot and rumpled, with Rollo sprawled across his shoulder like a small princely cloak. "He prefers the right side," Ragnar whispered, shifting the boy who was snoring into his beard. "If I try the left, he growls."

She laughed softly and leaned against him. "You were made for this," she said.

"I was made to hold heavy things," Ragnar said, "and he is very heavy in the ways that matter." He studied her profile. "How are you, my lightning.
Healing takes from a person, even when it gives."

Polyonymous looked at her hands. The skin around her knuckles glowed faintly, as if she had been holding moonlight and it had stained her. "I am well," she said. "Better than well. I used to think my power would always be the storm at the gate.

Maybe it is also the lamp someone places in a window when they are lost at sea."

Ragnar kissed her temple. "For the love of Odin's balls," he murmured, "marry me again when you talk like that."

By the fourth morning, Sigrid ran in the courtyard with a scarf tied around her head like a pirate queen. She shouted orders to invisible sailors and made Ragnar the cabin boy. He accepted the demotion with grace as long as Rollo was allowed to captain the ship from his arms. Leif watched, shaking his head in helpless joy.

When it was time for them to leave, Sigrid presented Polyonymous with a treasure she

had collected from the beach, a spiral shell the colour of dawn. "For calling the sea," she said solemnly. "In case it forgets where you live."

Polyonymous knelt and tucked the shell into the girl's palm again. "Keep it," she said. "Call me instead. If you need me, breathe slow and say my name three times. The wind will carry it."

Leif embraced Ragnar, then Polyonymous, then attempted to reclaim his son. Rollo clung to Ragnar's beard with both hands and made a sound that was not a word and yet meant no. After a negotiation that would have impressed any diplomat, Rollo agreed to leave only after Ragnar promised to visit before the first snow and to deliver a personal lecture on the art of growing a proper beard. Leif swore a blood oath to provide pears for that lecture.

The horses waited at the gate. Sigrid sat proudly in front of her father, her colour returned and her eyes bright. Rollo, entirely confident in his own importance, drooled on Leif's other shoulder. Before they rode out, Leif spoke so that the guards and the hall could hear him. "My house is bound to yours in gratitude," he said. "If you call, I will come."

They left, and the courtyard felt larger for the space they had occupied. Polyonymous stood very still.

The wind toyed with her hair, silver against the morning. Ragnar came to stand beside her. Together they watched the last of the riders disappear along the cliff road.

"You made a vow," Ragnar said. "Not only to Leif, but to yourself."

"I did," she said. "I will keep it." She turned
her palms up to the clean light. "I will be
lightning when I must, and I will be the small
blue flame that says, come home."

The sea answered in a quiet, contented way,
and the castle breathed with them. Far off,
dragons lifted their heads to the sky and tasted
the air that smelled like fennel, salt, and a
child's clean sleep.

Polyonymous gathered her tools and her shell
and went to prepare more remedies. There
would be other riders on other nights. She was
ready.

Interlude 8: Home in Niflheim

Polyonymous had not dream-walked in many moons, yet on this night her body gave itself fully to sleep.

The dream pulled her deeper, deeper, until the edges of waking dissolved and there was no other world, no other realm only this one.

She stood upon snow-laden cliffs, the wind biting, yet her heart whispered: Home. Truly home.
The air itself carried the scent of pine resin and frozen rivers, the wild essence of Niflheim.

And there he was.

Halsten, her love, her equal, her king. His towering figure moved with the certainty of one forged by winter storms.

His skin bore the blue of his people, shoulders broad as the gates of the castle, hair falling in silver-black waves.

When he smiled at her, the whole kingdom seemed to thaw.

"Come, my Queen," he said, his voice low thunder. "Steel dulls without use. Let us sharpen each other."

Steel rang against steel as they sparred. They circled each other on the training grounds, the snow beneath their boots crunching.

Polyonymous wielded her blade with precise grace, lightning sparking along its edge. Halsten's strikes were heavy and sure, the raw strength of glaciers in his arms. Blow met blow, sparks flew, and their laughter rose above the clamour.

"You cheat," Polyonymous teased, twisting free of his grip and landing a strike against his shoulder.

"And you tempt me, wife," Halsten replied, his grin fierce. "In war and in love, you are merciless."

They fought until sweat steamed from their skin despite the cold, until sparring blurred into embraces, until the kiss of blades became the kiss of lips.

And when the call to war came, they stood not against each other, but side by side two forces, one will, protecting their prosperous kingdom.

The Polar Bear

Not all of their journeys were on foot. At her side padded Þorri, the great polar bear, his armour gleaming with runes.
He had been gifted to her as a cub on the night of their wedding, a symbol of strength and loyalty.

Now, fully grown, he was massive, his paws striking thunder across the ice.
He shadowed her every step, guardian and companion, his white fur braided with silver charms that jingled softly in the wind.

When they travelled across mountains and valleys, Polyonymous often rode Þorri.
Snow falcons wheeled overhead, their keen eyes guiding the way through storms, their calls leading them back to the castle when the land lay cloaked in endless white.

The people of Niflheim would say: The Queen

does not walk alone. She walks with stormlight in her veins and a bear at her side.

Flashback – The Wedding Feast

The memory bloomed again, sharp as if it had happened only yesterday.

The great hall of Niflheim glowed with torchlight, the stone walls hung with banners of silver and blue.

On the dais, Halsten and Polyonymous sat as newly bound King and Queen, a polar bear cub nestled at Polyonymous' feet.
Þorri had yawned wide, showing teeth like carved ivory, before collapsing into her lap, already devoted.

"He is yours," Halsten had said, his voice carrying across the feast.

"A guardian who will know no master but you. A gift for my Queen who needs no guarding and yet, deserves to be guarded."

The hall roared with approval. Musicians struck their harps, drums thundered, and the people danced until the snow outside shook loose from the rooftops.

Hearth and Home

But her most treasured memories were not of war, nor ceremony, but of the quiet hours before the fire.

She and Halsten would stretch out upon a fur rug, boots kicked aside, weapons forgotten. They would play wooden games, moving pieces across carved boards, each accusing the other of cheating.

Halsten would grin slyly, slipping an extra piece forward. Polyonymous would catch him, laughing, and knock the board aside.

The game always ended with them tangled together, whispering jests and promises, feeding each other morsels of roasted meat and spiced wine.

It was then, of course, that the poor Chief of Arms would arrive every time.

"My King, my Queen," the man would cough awkwardly, eyes fixed anywhere but on them. "News of the watch. The eastern gates require reinforcement."

Halsten would groan, dramatically, still sprawled across the rug with Polyonymous pinned beneath his arm.

"My poor man," he said. "We should double his wages, wife. He endures far too much."

"Or buy him therapy," Polyonymous would tease, pressing her lips against Halsten's jaw as the man fled in red-faced silence.

Halsten's laughter had always rumbled against her skin like distant thunder.
"He knew what he was signing up for," he would reply, before pulling her closer into the warmth of firelight and love.

A Kingdom Guarded

Beyond their walls, there were threats. Raiders from the mountains tested their borders, and ice giants stirred in the northern valleys. Halsten and Polyonymous trained their people tirelessly. Together, they devised strategies, blending his strength with her foresight. On the field, they fought as a pair, Halsten's great axe sweeping arcs of destruction, Polyonymous' lightning strikes falling swift and precise.

Þorri roared through the fray, scattering foes like leaves before a storm.

After battles, they would walk the ramparts together, gazing out across the icefields.

Halsten's hand always found hers, rough and scarred yet gentle, grounding her in the present even as her seer's visions tugged her toward possible futures.

Closing

In the dream, all of it returned the battles, the bear, the fire, the love.

And Polyonymous, sinking deeper into that world, let herself believe she was still there. Still Halsten's queen. Still guarded by Þorri, still warmed by a love that burned hotter than any hearth.

And for once, she did not want to wake.

Chapter 23: Fire and Ice

The morning sun burned bright over the stone arena, its high walls ringing with the echo of steel on steel.

Ragnar and Polyonymous stood across from one another, blades drawn, their breath misting in the cold air.

Soldiers had gathered in the stands, eager to watch their King and Queen spar. Wagers were shouted, laughter rose, and every clang of metal echoed like thunder.

"Again," Ragnar barked, circling her with a wolf's grin. His axe gleamed, heavy and sure in his grip.

Polyonymous narrowed her eyes, lightning prickling faintly along her fingers even though she held only her sword.

"You'll regret asking for again, husband."

They clashed. Sparks flew where steel met steel, her strikes quick and precise, his strong and unrelenting.

The crowd roared as Polyonymous spun low, striking Ragnar's knee with the flat of her blade. He staggered, grinned wider, and swung his axe in a great arc. She ducked beneath it, laughing.

Above the noise came another sound high-pitched screeches, followed by a deafening crash.

Both Ragnar and Polyonymous froze mid-strike and turned toward the source.

At the edge of the arena, two dragons wreaked gleeful havoc.

Dreki, larger by far, had barrelled into the weapons rack, sending spears clattering across the stone.

Beside him, little Máni flapped her wings wildly, knocking over a water barrel with her tail.

The liquid spilled across the floor, soaking a cluster of soldiers who shouted in outrage. Dreki leapt onto the toppled spears as if they were his personal mountain, while Máni snatched a servant's tunic in her teeth and trotted proudly in circles.

The crowd erupted into laughter.

"Dreki!" Ragnar thundered.

"Máni!" Polyonymous scolded.

The dragons froze for three heartbeats before doubling their chaos. Dreki knocked over a shield rack, sending polished shields rolling like coins. Máni pounced on one and slid across the arena floor, squealing with delight.

Ragnar dragged a hand down his face. "They mock us, wife."

"They are your dragon kin, Ragnar perhaps they take after you." Polyonymous said dryly.

Before Ragnar could reply, Dreki spread his wings wide, chest puffed and let out a stream of red-orange fire.
The flames scorched the arena floor, licking dangerously close to the stands. Soldiers scrambled back, cheering and jeering.

Not to be outdone, Máni planted her tiny claws, inhaled deeply, and unleashed her own breath for the first time.

But it was not fire.

A jet of bright blue flame erupted from her maw, cold as the north wind. It struck Dreki square in the side and froze him solid.

The arena fell utterly silent.

Dreki's roar cut off in a muffled crackle of ice. His wings froze mid-flap, crystals glittering across every scale.
For a moment he looked like a statue carved from sapphire.

"By Odin's frozen balls," Ragnar breathed. "He's"

"Frozen Dreki," Polyonymous finished, wide-eyed.

Máni squealed in triumph, prancing about as if she had just won the entire kingdom. She snapped at the air, puffing tiny blue sparks that frosted over the arena floor. Soldiers laughed and pointed, though some looked uneasy.

Then the silence broke. The ice around Dreki began to glow. With a violent shudder, heat exploded outward.
Cracks spiderwebbed across the frozen prison until, with a furious roar, Dreki burst free. Molten fire streamed from his maw, melting the ice in a flood of steam.

The two dragons faced one another, smoke and frost curling between them.

The crowd gasped. The soldiers leaned forward, muttering.

Polyonymous exhaled slowly. "Ragnar… do you see?"

He nodded, awe breaking across his face. "A fire dragon… and an ice dragon. Both under one roof."

The soldiers erupted into cheers, stamping their feet. "Fire and Ice! Fire and Ice!" they chanted,
the sound rattling the stone arena.

As if to prove their titles, Dreki blasted a pillar with fire, while Máni puffed blue flame that froze a banner solid.
The banner snapped off its pole and shattered into icy shards. Laughter shook the stands.

One unlucky guard was frozen mid-speech as he tried to warn the Queen about safety measures. He stood in a block of frost, eyes wide, until Dreki's fire melted him free. The poor man stumbled away, soaked and steaming, to the sound of roaring applause.

Ragnar bent double, laughing. "By Odin's frozen balls, they'll bring the castle down before they're grown!"

Polyonymous raised her hands, lightning sparking at her fingertips. "They are balance," she said softly.
"Two sides of the storm."

Dreki and Máni, as if understanding, turned toward her and Ragnar, their eyes glowing with twin fires one of flame, one of frost. They bounded about the arena in renewed chaos, setting helmets ablaze and freezing shields solid. A knight's trousers caught fire only to be immediately frosted over by Máni, leaving the poor man squealing as steam hissed from his armour.

Ragnar threw an arm around his wife's shoulders, grinning like a man who had found treasure.

"Well, wife, we wanted to train this morning. Looks like we're raising our own battlefield instead."

Polyonymous smiled despite herself, leaning into him. "Yes. But perhaps it is the battlefield the gods meant for us to have."

The arena roared with chants as the dragons of fire and ice carved their legacy in steam and frost upon the stones.

Chapter 24: The Festival of Fire and Ice

The great square outside the castle was alive with colour, sound, and the smell of roasting meats. Banners of blue and red hung from every archway,
their silken tails snapping in the wind like tongues of flame and shards of ice. The people of the village and the castle had gathered in their thousands,
flooding the cobbled streets until they overflowed with laughter, song, and anticipation.

At the centre of it all sat Dreki and Máni.

The dragons had been scrubbed until their scales gleamed, Dreki's red-black hide glowing like banked embers, and Máni's pale blue-white scales

sparkling as though dusted with frost.
Children squealed as the great beasts stretched
their wings, casting wide shadows over the
square.
Instead of fleeing in fear as they once had, the
people ran forward with baskets of offerings
fish fresh from the sea, rabbits fattened from
the fields,
and haunches of goat meat that still steamed
from the fire.

"Step forward, step forward," Ragnar called,
his booming voice echoing over the crowd. He
stood with an axe slung at his hip,
though his smile was wide and his eyes proud.
"Bring honour to our guardians of Fire and
Ice!"

The line of villagers shuffled forward, each one
bowing before placing their gifts upon a great
stone trough set between the dragons.

Dreki plunged his head into the pile first, snapping up an entire goat leg with one crunch. Beside him, Máni delicately plucked a fish from the heap, tossing it into the air before swallowing it whole.

Polyonymous laughed softly as she watched from the dais. She wore her Queen's circlet, but her hands were clasped in front of her like a mother watching two unruly children. "They are in heaven," she murmured.

"Aye," Ragnar said, resting a hand on her shoulder. "But give them ten breaths and they'll find mischief again."

As if summoned by his words, Dreki's tail lashed out and upended a barrel of mead. The golden liquid splashed across the cobbles, sending villagers diving to save their cups. Máni chirped gleefully and crouched low, lapping at the spreading pool until her snout dripped sticky foam.

Dreki butted her aside with a huff, and soon the two were wrestling in the middle of the square, scattering offerings in every direction.

"By Odin's balls," Ragnar muttered, though his grin betrayed his amusement.

The crowd laughed and cheered. Children clapped their hands and chanted the dragons' names, while elders shook their heads but smiled nonetheless.

Later, when the square had quieted and the sun dipped low, the elders of the realm gathered in the council chamber.

Polyonymous and Ragnar sat at the head of the

long table, Dreki and Máni curled outside the tall windows, their snores rumbling like distant thunder.

An old man with a staff of oak leaned forward. "Majesties," he began, "the dragons are no longer pests to be shooed from the granaries. They are honoured by the people. Loved, even. But love alone will not guide them."

An elder woman, her braids bound with silver thread, nodded. "They are strong already. Too strong to be left untended.
If they are to grow unchecked, they may one day see the kingdom as a nest to claim rather than a home to protect."

Ragnar's hand tightened on the table. "You think they would turn on us?"

"No," the woman said gently. "Not now. But

wild blood is dangerous if not tempered with purpose."

Another elder raised his voice. "We propose they be trained. Not as beasts, but as guardians of the realm.
Let them grow knowing discipline, as your warriors do. Teach them that their fire and frost are for defence, not mischief."

Polyonymous's eyes softened. She looked through the window at Máni, the little dragoness curled in the crook of Dreki's wing. "And how would you have us train them?"

The answer came from the scholar at the end of the table. His robes smelled of parchment and ink, and his eyes gleamed with ideas.

"There are ways to open the bridge between dragon and rider. Ways to teach them to speak mind-to-mind.

With your blessing, we could begin the art of telepathic communion. At first, their voices would be clumsy images, feelings, fragments.

But with time, you would hear their thoughts as clearly as speech."

Ragnar's brows shot up. "You mean to say I'll have Dreki yammering in my head all day?"

The room rippled with restrained laughter.

Polyonymous hid a smile behind her hand. "It would mean we understand them better. That they are not left guessing at us, nor we at them."

The scholar inclined his head. "And more. We would suggest fitting them with armour, even now, while they are young.

Let them grow accustomed to the weight, the feel of steel upon their scales.
Better they learn to bear it with ease than resent it when battle calls."

Another elder added, "And their breaths. Fire and ice must be tempered. They must learn control when to use them, and when to hold back. If they are guardians, they cannot terrify the very people they are sworn to protect."

Silence fell. Ragnar leaned back in his chair, fingers stroking his beard as he studied his Queen.
Polyonymous met his gaze, the storm-light flickering faintly in her eyes.

"Well, wife?" he asked. "Do we make warriors of them?"

Polyonymous looked once more at the

dragons, their slumber peaceful, their bodies still so small beside the weight of destiny. She felt the spark of fate tug in her chest, the whisper of the gods on the wind.

"They are already warriors," she said softly. "But let us make them guardians too. Not wild storms but storms with a purpose."

Ragnar grinned, slamming his palm on the table. "So be it! The Fire and the Ice shall be the realm's shield as well as its terror."

The elders bowed their heads in agreement. Plans were set in motion that night of lessons in discipline, of armour to be forged, and of scholars who would teach the language of minds.

Outside the window, Dreki stirred in his sleep, sparks curling from his nostrils. Beside him,

Máni shifted and exhaled a small puff of blue
frost
that froze the grass at her feet. Even in dreams,
fire and ice danced together.

And so the kingdom's greatest guardians
began their path not as beasts to be feared, but
as legends in the making.

Chapter 25: River of Rainbows and Ruckus

Morning cracked open like a bright yolk over the harbor, spilling gold across the water and painting the masts in fire.

Two valcory ships, sleek, rune-etched river-cutters with high swan prows rocked in their berths, rigging humming in the sea breeze.

On the quay, sailors hurried with coils of rope and wicker baskets, castle staff lugged hampers that smelled of honeyed breads and smoked fish,

and a very large Minotaur adjusted an even larger breastplate while pretending he did not enjoy the admiring stares.

"Chief of Armies," Ragnar called, slapping the Minotaur's plated shoulder. "If the wind rises, your horns may take us airborne."

Bjorn tossed his thick mane and snorted politely. "If the wind rises, my King, your beard will act as a sail, and we'll make better time."

Polyonymous hid a smile as she secured the last of the salves and storm-phials in a leather satchel. "Play nice," she said, voice warm. "We have dragons to train and thunder to coax. I would prefer not to fish either of you from the river."

At her heels pranced Máni, the blue-white dragoness, bright as moonlit ice; on the railing, Dreki crouched with a crackle of ember-red scales
and a look that suggested the world was his chew toy. The harbor folk growing bolder by the day waved and whooped, tossing fish to the little beasts
as offerings. Dreki gulped his in one snap.

Máni batted hers into the air, let it glimmer, then slurped it down with princess dignity.

Ragnar caught Polyonymous around the waist, mischief in his eyes. "Ready, my lightning?"

"Always," she said, pressing her brow to his. "Let's give the day a story."

They cast off under banners that flashed red and blue, Fire and Ice, and the valcory ships slid into the river like knives into silk.
The kingdom's waterways braided the land into a tapestry: emerald meadows stitched to onyx cliffs, green and black mountains rising like the backs of sleeping gods.
Rainbows arched high and repeated themselves in the spray one, two, three, stacked like gates to a palace of light.

Bjorn stood midships with a long ash stave, his hooves planted, tail swishing, an instructor carved of myth and muscle.

"Formations!" he bellowed. "We drill the pair, then the single. Dreki, on my left. Máni, on the Queen's right. Ragnar, keep your head down when I say release.

Last time you nearly lost an eyebrow."

Ragnar smirked. "I have two. Spare parts."

"Noted," Bjorn said. "Try not to set them both on fire."

Polyonymous closed her eyes and let the river wind thread her braid. She lifted her hands, fingers loose, runes a murmur on her tongue. The storm answered her like an attentive hound ears pricked, waiting for a sign. Not rage this time. Precision.

"First pass," Bjorn barked. "Low flare, short stream. On my mark release!"

Dreki inhaled, chest swelling, and let loose a neat ribbon of red-orange flame that licked the river's skin without boiling it.
Steam rose like applause. On the other ship's bow, Ragnar whooped and slapped the railing. "That's my boy!"

"Second," Bjorn said, turning, "ice flare. Short, steady. Máni, release."

The dragoness's blue fire came out as a cone of silver frost that glazed a patch of water into crystal. The ship sliced through it;
the ice shattered into shards that glittered like thrown jewels.

Polyonymous laughed, delighted. "Good girl. Thought and breath together." She stroked

Máni's neck; the dragon purred so loudly the hull vibrated.

"Again," Bjorn commanded, pleased but merciless. "We chain them fire left, ice right then the Queen's strike through the seam."

They drilled. Fire. Ice. Polyonymous threading lightning like silver stitching between them, splitting steam with clean white cracks that rumbled and rolled away into the mountains. Each pass grew smoother. Each command, sharper. The crew learned when to duck, when to lean, when to clap and when to extinguish a smouldering rope with a bucket and a prayer.

Midmorning, a gust shoved them through a narrow throat of canyon where black cliffs leaned close as gossiping aunts. Mist haloed the prows; the river narrowed to a quick bright blade.

"Hold steady," Bjorn warned, bracing. "No drama."

Which, of course, summoned drama.

A pair of river-stags bounded across a stone bridge overhead. Dreki, ecstatic, reared on the railing to greet his new best friends and, ffft… accidentally burped a spark.
One singe. Two curls. Ragnar patted out a smoking tuft of beard and gave his dragon a look of tragic betrayal.

"By Odin's frozen balls," he muttered. "The beard again."

Máni, affronted on behalf of good grooming, hopped to the rail and blew a small, earnest puff of blue. Ragnar's beard and eyebrows frosted over instantly, stiff as sugared fruit.

Even his lashes.

Silence. Then Bjorn, voice reverent: "Majesties, winter has come… to your face."

Polyonymous made a small, strangled sound. "Bjorn," she said, failing to sound stern, "you would mock your King's misfortune?"

Bjorn's ears dipped. "Respectfully, my Queen… yes."

They looked at each other for half a heartbeat and collapsed both of them into helpless laughter. Ragnar tried to glower,
but every blink shook a flurry of ice crystals into the air like celebratory confetti, and that did not help.

He hooked an arm around Polyonymous, pulling her close, laughter still in his chest.

"You, my Queen, are encouraging him to mutiny."

"I am encouraging joy," she said, eyes shining. She rose on her toes and kissed the frost from his lashes. He kissed her brow in return, soft and sure, and she because this was a day that asked for boldness kissed him back on the mouth, lingering until the crew whooped and Dreki chirped and Máni fanned her wings like a scandalized aunt.

"Break," Bjorn announced, magnificently unbothered. "Before the King freezes solid."

They brought the ships to shore in a meadow bright with buttercups and starflowers. The castle staff had outdone themselves: three hampers of warm barley loaves, a wheel

of hard white cheese, jars of pickled sea-lilies,
spiced nuts, pears folded in leaves,
smoked trout with lemon, honey cakes glazed
to the shine of moons. A skin of mead, a skin of
water, and, by the look Bjorn gave a third skin,
something that could fell an ox.

They sprawled on wool blankets. Dreki and
Máni curled like enormous house cats at the
edge of the picnic, each presented with a
mound approved of fish and goat.

Polyonymous sliced bread and tucked cheese
into it for Ragnar, who pretended he was too
warrior to accept it until she raised a brow.
Then he accepted it like a supplicant receiving
sacrament.

"Training note," Bjorn said between
mouthfuls. "Dreki's lateral control is better. He
can hold a narrow beam now.

Máni's frost is over-generous she loves to paint
the whole world blue. We'll teach her the
difference between 'lace the window' and
'glacier the cathedral'."

Polyonymous nodded. "We can anchor with
posture cues. A tap behind the jaw to narrow,
palm to chest to widen.
And I'll thread a soft thunder hum when I
want them to hold breath rather than release."

Ragnar, mouth full, offered: "And I will stand
far away from my own beard."

"Sound doctrine," Bjorn said gravely.

The dragons ate daintily (Máni) and not at all
daintily (Dreki). A butterfly landed on Máni's
nose; she crossed her eyes, sneezed a
snowflake,
and watched it tumble away with such pride

you'd think she'd invented weather. Dreki, not
to be outdone, discovered that if he huffed on
honey cake first,
it caramelized. He then attempted to
caramelize all the honey cakes, forcing Ragnar
to institute a brisk policy of "No, not that one,
give, give Dreki, that's my lunch."

They lay back after, bellies full, watching the
high river clouds knit a shawl across the sun.
Polyonymous laced her fingers behind her
head and listened to the faint hum of the storm
lingering in her bones.
It was a soft thing today, a pulse more than a
roar. The kind of electricity that makes a cat's
fur stand when a hand passes above it.

"Ready for the Queen's strikes?" Bjorn asked,
rolling to his hooves with an agility that
surprised everyone who forgot he was half
bull, half thunderbolt.

"I want twelve clean canopies, gentle enough to spare birds, strong enough to frighten raiders into confession."

Polyonymous stood, brushing flowers from her skirt. "Twelve," she agreed. "And a baker's dozen if you compliment Ragnar's beard."

Bjorn eyed the frosted masterpiece. "My Queen, it's… inspiring. A tundra one could get lost in."

Ragnar sighed tragically. "He means lovely," Polyonymous translated, and Ragnar, mollified, kissed her knuckles.

They sailed again under a chorus of larks. The river widened, breathing deeper. Bjorn set targets floating shields tethered to driftwood, a line of painted buoys, a cluster of smoke pots that would tell the wind's mood by how the plumes leaned.

"Sequence," he commanded. "Dreki low burn, kiss the first shield. Máni feather frost, filigree the second. Queen thread the seam with thunder, then disperse the smoke to clear the valley."

The world narrowed. Dreki's beam drew a charcoal smile across the old bronze. Máni's blue stitched lace across iron, white veining that shone then sublimated into mist. Polyonymous lifted her hands and felt lightning gather not the spear of wrath, but the musician's sustained note.
She sent it in a clean line, zznn… between fire and frost. The smoke pots, obedient as courtiers, bowed and opened the valley like a curtain.

The crew cheered. Even the river seemed to clap against the hulls.

"Again," Bjorn said, always the taskmaster. "A little faster. Add a roll."

They danced their strange ballet all afternoon: dragons and Queen and King and Minotaur, ships and river, sun and rainbow.
Sailors learned to read the dragons' shoulders. Dragons learned to read Bjorn's tail. Ragnar learned where his beard should not be.

Only once did the day threaten itself. A squall rolled down a far peak, cold enough to bite. The rainbow above them brightened and split, its double swelling to triple, to quadruple an impossible crown of light.

"Stormlet," Polyonymous said, eyes narrowing. "May I?"

Bjorn looked to Ragnar; Ragnar looked to her; together they nodded.

She stepped to the prow and called the clouds by their quieter names. The lightning she summoned was a whisper, a slender reed, a thread she wove through the thunder's loom. It struck the stormlet's heart and unspooled it like a spool of dark. The rain it meant to empty fell instead as luminous pins that melted before they touched the deck.
The rainbow collapsed to one perfect arc that settled like a blessing over both valcory ships.

"Show-off," Ragnar murmured, awed.

"To be fair," Bjorn said, "if I could embroider the sky, I would."

Polyonymous turned, cheeks pinked by the

wind. "Consider it practice. Someday the sky may not be in a mood to be polite."

"Then we will be ready," Bjorn promised.

They turned for home as the sun slipped toward its red bed. The river widened into the low marshy skirts of the kingdom; reeds whispered, and frogs tuned their evening orchestra.

Dreki yawned a curl of smoke and curled at the foredeck, chin on paws. Máni curled into him, a crescent of blue against a hearth of red, their breaths syncing warm, cool, warm, cool like a bellows that never tired.

On shore, they made a small camp in the lee of a willow. Sailors set a tidy fire; cooks warmed a last pot of stew; someone sang a simple rowing song that sounded like home.

Bjorn took first watch without being asked, leaned his broad back against the tree, and cleaned his axe with the tender focus of a parent braiding a child's hair.

Ragnar spread a thick fur by the fire and tugged Polyonymous gently down. "Today was a good day," he said quietly, the bluster gone, the man beneath all the gleam and jokes.

"It was," she agreed, resting her head on his shoulder. "We asked the dragons to be more than marvellous, and they were. We asked the storm to be kinder, and it listened."

"Bjorn will put the fear of discipline into all of us tomorrow," he said, smiling into her hair.

"I will let him," she said. "He is good for us."

A soft chirrup. They looked over. Máni had nosed closer to the fire until her whiskers warmed. She made a small, satisfied sound and went still again.

Dreki, three heartbeats later, figured out the exact boundary between cozy and singe and set his chin there, immensely proud.

Ragnar's arm tightened around Polyonymous. "You, my Queen, are encouraging my chief of armies to mock me and my dragons to roast me."

"I am encouraging love to look like laughter," she murmured. She tilted her face up. He kissed her forehead, worship quiet. She kissed him back on the mouth, unhurried, a benediction more than a battle cry.

The fire settled. The reeds sang. Bjorn's silhouette was a steady mountain against the willow. Somewhere, far off, the sea turned in its sleep and sighed.

Polyonymous drifted first, the last of the storm
humming soft in her bones. Ragnar followed,
his breath a warm rope around her.
The dragons, fireside, dreamed: of caramelized
honey cakes, of snowflakes and sparks, of
rainbows that could be chased and caught.

And the kingdom dreamed with them of a
road braided by riverlight, of guardians who
were learning, of a day that had been both jest
and vow.

By morning, there would be drills and plans
and armour fittings and scholars with careful
voices. But for now, under the willow and the
faithful watch of a Minotaur,
Fire and Ice slept beside one another, and the
night kept its promise: to keep what it loved
safe.

Interlude 9: The Dream of Loss, the Promise of Storms

The night was hushed, the kind of stillness that makes every torch crackle louder, every heartbeat seem too loud.

In their private chamber, the furs were pulled up against the cold, the fire casting golden lines across stone walls.

Polyonymous stood at the window, gazing out at the snow-blanketed mountains, her robe slipping from her shoulders.

Behind her, strong arms slid into the folds of fabric, drawing it back around her. A kiss brushed her neck, then another, slow and reverent.

"Halsten…" she whispered, her breath trembling like the flames on the hearth.

"My queen," he rumbled, voice low enough to be mistaken for the mountain's own growl, "no night is worthy unless you are clothed in my devotion."

She turned, her smile soft and almost shy despite the fire in her veins. He took her hands and guided her to the carved chair near the fire.
She sat, letting the robe slip open just enough for warmth and comfort, and pressed a brush into his waiting hand.

Halsten took the brush as though it were a sacred relic. He began to work it gently through her dark hair, each stroke smooth and unhurried.
She closed her eyes, a faint purr leaving her lips, and when his broad fingers began to braid three strands on one side, three on the other her whole body melted into bliss.

"You spoil me," she murmured, kissing his hand when he paused.

"You deserve spoiling," he replied, finishing the last braid and laying it over her shoulder. He leaned down and kissed the crown of her head, then pulled her against his chest, hard and unyielding as carved stone.

"You, my queen, are worthy of my worship."

Her cheeks burned, but she let herself sink deeper into his embrace, the weight of his words and his arms wrapping around her like armour.

Dawn came sharp and cold, the kind of morning that promised blood on snow. Horns echoed through the keep, summoning their armies.

From the highest balcony, Polyonymous and Halsten looked down upon their host ranks of shieldmaidens and warriors, snow falcons tethered to gauntlets, axes glinting in the early light.

Beside them stood Þorri, her great polar bear, armour strapped across his white shoulders, his breath steaming like a forge.

A scout bowed low. "The Viking humans gather in the lower grounds. Their numbers swell, and they drive beasts before them. If they grow unchecked, our supplies will dwindle, and our borders will be threatened."

Halsten's jaw set like granite. "Then we stop them today."

Polyonymous rested her hand on Þorri's fur, nodding. "Together."

The army moved through the mountains, boots

crunching over ice, banners snapping in the wind.

The path narrowed into switchbacks, but they pressed onward until they reached the high ground above the valley.

Below, like ants seething across snow, the Viking humans massed, their weapons glinting and their beasts snarling.

Halsten raised a hand, signalling silence. They would strike from above, the mountain itself their ally.

The first horn blast shattered the stillness, and the army descended. Shields locked, arrows sang, falcons streaked down like silver lightning.

Þorri thundered beside Polyonymous, a wall of white fury, his roar echoing like avalanches.

Halsten was at the front, sword raised high, his

presence undeniable, his charge a storm given flesh. Beside him, Polyonymous ran, her heart hammering,
her hands itching for the lightning she so often commanded. But when she reached for it nothing. The skies were silent, her power stripped from her as though the dream itself forbade her strength.

And then she saw them.

The Viking king stepped forward, towering and terrible, his helm crowned with horns. And when his face came into view, her heart stopped it was Ragnar.

Her Ragnar.

And flanking him were two dragons: Dreki, scales blazing like embers, and Máni, her icy shimmer piercing the white storm.

"No…" Polyonymous gasped, stumbling. Her heart slammed against her ribs, threatening to break free.

Halsten didn't pause. His massive sword swung once, twice effortless arcs of death. With the first stroke, Dreki's head fell, rolling in fire across the snow.

With the second, Máni crumpled, her scales shattering into a thousand frozen shards. And with a final, brutal thrust, Halsten drove his blade into Ragnar's chest.

Polyonymous screamed, the sound tearing from her throat like her soul itself was being ripped apart. She lunged forward, powerless, only to see Ragnar fall,
his blood steaming on the snow, his eyes dimming as he reached for her.
"NO!"

Her scream echoed until the battlefield
dissolved, the world collapsing into shadow.

Polyonymous bolted upright, sweat damp on
her brow. The bed was familiar, the chamber
warm, but her heart still raced with terror.
She threw the furs aside and ran barefoot
through the castle halls, her braid unravelling
as she went.

She found Ragnar in the training yard. He
stood with a barrel of nuts, laughing as he
tossed them one by one into the air.
Dreki leapt, roasting them mid-flight with
bursts of fire, while Máni followed with precise
streams of frost, freezing them before they hit
the ground.
The courtyard was littered with half-roasted,
half-frozen nuts, a battlefield of comedy.

Ragnar looked up, eyebrows singed slightly from Dreki's enthusiasm, and grinned. "You see, my love? Dinner and entertainment! Who needs jesters when you have dragons?"

She didn't answer. Instead, she ran forward, flinging her arms around Dreki, kissing his warm, scaly forehead, then Máni's cool snout. Only then did she climb into Ragnar's lap, clutching him as though he might vanish.

"I had a terrible nightmare," she whispered, tears in her eyes. "In the high mountains, where we were to march… you and the dragons died. All of our armies fell. I saw it. I *felt* it."

Ragnar's laughter faded, his arms tightening around her. He kissed her temple, serious now.

"I had already planned to leave tomorrow. We cannot let those raiders roam unchecked.
But if what you dreamed is true, then we must act quickly. We will face them before they grow stronger."

Polyonymous shook her head, firm. "Then I am coming with you. For in this reality…" She raised her hand, sparks of lightning dancing across her fingertips.

"…my storm is mine to command. And I will not let death take you."

Ragnar studied her, pride and love blazing in his eyes. He kissed her, long and steady, then whispered against her lips:

"Then let us make your dream a lie, and our victory the truth."

The dragons roared, one of fire, one of frost,

their voices twining as though to seal the vow.

286

Chapter 26: The Two Kings and the Falling Mountain

The mountains rumbled like giants waking in their sleep. Snow slipped down black stone cliffs, and echoes rolled through the gorge like drums.

Polyonymous stood at the edge, her braid whipping in the wind, lightning snapping across her fingertips. She had not slept since the nightmare, not truly.
The image of Ragnar and the dragons falling before Halsten's blade had carved itself into her bones. And she knew if the two kings ever met, blood would follow.

She whispered to herself, steady and fierce, "I will not let either of them die. I will not let my worlds collide."

Her plan was simple in theory and reckless in practice: seal the gorge. The Viking humans would never march into Niflheim if the valley itself became their tomb.

She lifted her arms to the storm, calling it with the old words. Thunder answered, rolling low, the kind of growl that makes the heart trip. A bolt cracked from her palms, blasting into the cliffside. Rock exploded outward, avalanching into the gorge. Another strike. Another blast.

"Stay calm," she muttered, voice trembling as sparks lit the sky. "Just a little more"

But the storm had other ideas. Lightning poured from her like floodwater, wild and merciless. The mountain shook. Rocks toppled in great slabs,
dust pluming high, the air tasting of ozone and

terror.

From opposite sides of the valley, two armies stopped in their tracks.

Halsten, towering on his war bear Þorri, shaded his eyes. "By the gods, that's my little queen WAIT. Why is there lightning coming from her hands?"

Across the gorge, Ragnar stood frozen, Dreki and Máni at his side, both dragons wide-eyed. "By Odin's frozen balls," he muttered. "She's going to bring the whole mountain down on her head!"

As if on cue, a boulder the size of a longhouse cracked loose, shattered, and struck the ledge where she stood. The world went white with dust.

Polyonymous toppled, arms limp and

vanished under the falling rocks.

"POLYONYMOUS!" both kings roared, their voices colliding in thunder.

They charged.

Halsten reached her first, his massive frame hurling rocks aside like they were children's toys. His hands found her, limp but breathing, her pulse a fragile drum under his calloused fingers. He cradled her against his chest, brushing stone-dust from her face.

"My queen," he whispered, voice shaking. "Stay with me. Stay."

Boots pounded behind him. Ragnar stormed up the slope, ice still clinging to his beard from Máni's nervous puff.
He drew his sword, eyes blazing.

"Unhand my Queen and my Wife!" he
demanded.

Halsten turned, wide-eyed, still clutching her.
"Your wife? This is my wife, little man."

Ragnar arched one brow. "Who are you calling
little? I am of every acceptable warrior-king
size!
And I will have you unhand my wife at once,
you beast!"

Halsten squinted, unimpressed. "No, she is my
wife and Queen. I think you have had one too
many drinks, your tiny king!"

Ragnar staggered, scandalized. "Tiny?! Oh no,
Dream Boy, I assume."

Halsten stiffened. "Who are you calling Dream
Boy?"

Ragnar jabbed a finger at him. "This is Polyonymous. She is my queen and wife, and every night she walks in dreams. You're not the first king she's visited, you know."

Halsten blinked. "What are you saying, you strange little Viking man?"

"I am saying" Ragnar growled, "you're not even her first. Let's get her somewhere safe, and I can tell you all about her dream walking. She needs tending, not two men bellowing over her like oxen at a market."

Halsten growled back but finally nodded. "Fine. But we take her to my castle in Niflheim. Your army must leave. They are not welcome there."

Ragnar crossed his arms, chin high. "I will

send them back. But the dragons come with
me."

Halsten narrowed his eyes. "Fine. But they do
not shed fire or frost in my halls."

"Agreed," Ragnar said.

Both men glared another heartbeat, then
looked down at the unconscious queen in
Halsten's arms.
For her, for now, there would be truce.

Ragnar ordered his army back with a wave.
His men grumbled, confused, but obeyed.
Dreki and Máni padded after him,
their scales glowing faintly, eyes locked on
Polyonymous with soft, worried chirps.
Halsten, still carrying her as if she were a
crown too fragile to set down, mounted Þorri.

Ragnar climbed onto Dreki,
muttering about how ridiculous it was to have
to ride after his wife in another man's arms.

"Try not to drop her, Dream Boy," Ragnar
called.

Halsten snorted. "Try not to fall off your
overgrown lizard, Tiny King."

And so, with thunder muttering in the sky and
dragons snorting behind, the strangest
procession Niflheim had ever seen began its
march to Halsten's castle.

Behind them, the gorge lay sealed, a scar across
the mountains. Neither Ragnar's nor Halsten's
men could cross.
The armies had been spared their clash, but the
real battle was only just beginning.

For in the halls of Niflheim, two kings and one
queen would soon have to face the truth:
that love, loyalty, and lightning can set even
the strongest hearts to war.

Chapter 27: The Two Kings' Truce

The chamber smelled of pine smoke and honeyed herbs. Light from the hearth flickered soft and gold, casting shadows across fur-draped walls.

Polyonymous lay still on a bed of furs, her hair splayed out like a crown of night, her breathing faint but steady. Healers had worked in silence for hours,

pressing poultices, chanting old words, burning incense that curled into patterns only the gods could read. At last they left, bowing their heads.

"Her fate," one had whispered, "rests in the hands of the old gods."

And so, the room was left guarded by three warriors who did not trust one another in the

slightest: a war-bear, a fire dragon, and an ice
dragon.

Þorri lay like a fortress beside her, snout
tucked against his paws, golden eyes never
leaving the queen. Dreki and Máni crept close
again and again,
eager to nuzzle or slobber over their mistress.
Each time, Þorri lifted one enormous paw
without so much as opening his eyes. The
message was clear: try me.

The dragons chirped, puffed, even staged an
elaborate act where Dreki pretended to limp so
that Þorri might chase him. The bear didn't so
much as twitch.
Máni sighed, flopped onto her back
dramatically, and blew a puff of blue frost into
the air, freezing one of the chandeliers.
The icicles rained down, narrowly missing
Ragnar's head.

"By Odin's frozen balls," Ragnar muttered, brushing shards from his beard. "Even in grief, they try to kill me."

Halsten, arms folded, rumbled low. "They show devotion in their own way. They love her."

"They slobber," Ragnar countered. "There is a difference."

The silence stretched. The only sounds were the crackle of fire and the faint snores of Þorri. Ragnar leaned back in his chair, the weight of days settling into his shoulders.
He looked across the room at Halsten, who stood like a carved monolith, hands on the hilt of his sword.

"We must speak," Ragnar said.

Halsten arched a brow. "King to king?"

"King to king," Ragnar confirmed, stroking his beard. "No fists, no axes. Words."

Halsten eased into the opposite chair. For a moment, they looked more like drinking companions than rivals, until Ragnar opened his mouth.

"She came to me first," Ragnar began, "as my queen, my wife. It is not a boast. It is truth. She walks between dreams, Halsten. I did not ask it, but it is so.
And in each dream, she has found a king."

Halsten frowned, his gaze flicking to Polyonymous's still form. "A dangerous gift. Tell me everything."
And Ragnar did. He spoke of The Stone-Kissed King of Jötunheim, who had given her his

crown of rock. Of The Tidal Prince and The Shadowbound,

who had tempted her across waves and shadows. Of Huldra, the Elf King of Alfheim, radiant in light. Of The Sea King's Warning, when the waters themselves had roared against her. Of The Child and the Storm in Asgard, a boy crowned too young. Of The Frost Dream,

where an ice king had called her sister of storms. Of The Fire King, who burned brighter than reason in Muspelheim. And finally, of Halsten himself, her fierce love in Niflheim.

For a long time, Halsten said nothing. His jaw clenched, then unclenched, like a mountain trying not to crack. He rose, pacing the chamber.

His shadow fell over the fur bed, over the

dragons, over Ragnar.

"So," Halsten said at last, his voice sharp as breaking ice, "you mean to tell me… my Queen has so far been to, "

He ticked them off on his fingers, each word a hammer strike.

"Jötunheim: a Rock Giant King."
"Svaralfheim: a Dark Elf Princes."
"Alfheim: An Elf King of Light."
"Vanaheim: The Sea King."
"Asgard: a child on the throne."
"Jötunheim again: an Ice King."
"Muspelheim: A Fire King."
"And me… Halsten, King of Niflheim."

He stopped pacing. His eyes blazed with something Ragnar had never seen before: fear.

"That is eight of the nine realms," Halsten said hoarsely. "Eight. The only one left is Hel."

Both men turned to look at her, lying silent in the furs. The fire hissed low. A chill swept the room.

Ragnar's mouth, for once, had no jest left in it. "Hel," he repeated softly, and the word itself seemed to curdle the air. "If she walks there…"

Halsten's voice dropped to a growl. "If she walks there, she may never return."

The silence pressed heavy. Ragnar shifted, the colour draining from his cheeks. "By Thor's sagging goat balls," he muttered, "we may have already lost her."

Halsten grunted agreement. For the first time, they looked not as rivals, but as two men who loved the same woman and feared the same gods.

At last, Halsten dropped to one knee. His massive frame bent low, he pressed his forehead to the floor. Ragnar stared at him, astonished.

"You pray?" Ragnar asked, incredulous.

Halsten's voice was gravel. "I would wrestle the world itself for her. But in this… only the old gods may decide."

Ragnar hesitated, then, with an awkward sigh, knelt beside him. "I'm not much for kneeling. Makes the knees creak. But for her…" He cleared his throat, looking skyward.

"Oi! Old gods! If you're listening, this would be a good time to wake up and pay attention."

Halsten shot him a glare, but Ragnar pressed

on.

"Bring her back," Ragnar said, quieter now. "Bring our queen back. She belongs with us not in Hel."

Halsten's hand tightened on his sword hilt. "Let her storm be ours again."

The fire guttered. The air trembled. Dreki and Máni lifted their heads and hummed, voices strange and solemn. Even Þorri opened one golden eye, as if the old gods themselves had leaned close to listen.

And so, in that chamber of firelight and furs, two kings who had sworn to kill each other bowed instead to the unseen, begging for the return of one woman who bound them both. Whether the gods would listen… remained a mystery.

Interlude 10: The Ninth Door

The cave breathed.

It was a slow, tidal breath, a pull and push of cool air that smelled of salt and iron, as if the sea itself slept somewhere deeper inside the rock.

Polyonymous stood at the threshold, fingers grazing the damp stone, trying to remember whether she had walked here or been woven here by a dream she had not agreed to. The world behind her was black.

The world ahead was black. Only the hush of water and the thin silver thread of her own breath marked the place where she stood.

"Hello?" she called, voice swallowed by the cavern.

No answer, only that patient tide breathing in the dark.

A glow stirred far within, faint as foxfire at first, then steadying into the warm, pale-gold light of a lantern. A woman's figure stepped through it, light around her like a cloak. She was tall. Bare feet. The hem of her dress left wet crescents on the floor with every step, and with each drop Polyonymous felt that odd sea-smell grow stronger, briny and old.

"Hello," Polyonymous tried again, softer. "I am Polyonymous. Can you tell me where I am. Can you help me."

The woman came close enough that the glow painted her face. Her eyes were the colour of storm glass pulled from a wreck, and little shells and bones hung in her hair, clicking softly as if they still remembered waves.

"I can," the woman said. "And I will."

"What is your name."

"I am Rán."

The name moved like a current through the cave. Somewhere far off, water sighed.

"And yes," Rán added, "I can help you. I am the guide in this realm. But there is a price to be paid before I can help."

Polyonymous set her jaw. "What is the price."

"Ten pieces of gold."

It was not the cruel price she had braced for, the kind demanded by tricksters and petty kings. She loosened the cord of her Birka coin bag and counted ten bright circles into her palm. The coins sang softly, metal on metal, and that song echoed down the stone ribs of the cave as she pressed them into Rán's hand.

Rán weighed them, then let them fall into the pocket of the sea as if there were a pocket there. "Welcome to the Ninth Realm," she said. "I will assist your way to Hel. She can give you more answers than I may."

"You say Ninth Realm as if this is a place with doors in every direction."

Rán's smile showed the edge of a wave before it breaks. "It is. Keep close. The currents here do not forgive a wandering step."

A golden boat waited on black water at the cave's lip, a valkyrie craft shaped like a swan with its neck bowed. When Polyonymous

climbed in, the boat rocked once and steadied
beneath her. Rán did not take oar or rudder.
She put one bare foot upon the prow and the
boat moved, as if the sea bent to her footfall.

They sailed into darkness that thickened
around them until the boat and the women in
it were a mote in pitch. The glow that held to
Rán became the only rule left in the world. The
water was without wave, a mirror that did not
reflect. Sound fell away, leaving only the slow,
distant thud of something like a heart, though
whether it was the world's or her own,
Polyonymous could not tell.
"How long is the passage," Polyonymous
asked once, because the long quiet had started
to gather questions in her chest like stones.

"Longer than you like," Rán said. "Shorter
than you fear."

"Not helpful."

"Then take the helpful truth. There is no time here, only choice. We arrive when you are ready to meet who waits."

The cave narrowed to a throat of stone, then opened without warning into a vault so large the light reached and failed and reached again, climbing pillars and ribs of rock like the inside of some giant's cathedral. At the far end, a pair of gates stood not as doors but as a verdict, iron grown out of the bedrock, carved with beasts that had never known sunlight. The boat kissed a ledge of slate.

Rán stepped out and offered her hand.

Polyonymous climbed after her. Iron sliders groaned. The gates pulled back.

A hall lay beyond, long and low, lit by oil lamps set in bowls of bone. Firelight walked the walls. The air was warmer, but it carried a new scent now, not the simple salt of the sea, but something older, the hush of dust and ash, a sweetness like myrrh left too long on a shrine.

Rán guided her along the rocky passage without speaking. When they reached a chamber with a high door of polished black wood, Rán stopped.

"

I will go no further," she said. "My waters end here. Her road begins."

Polyonymous touched Rán's wrist. "Thank you."

"Keep the coin you did not spend," Rán said gently. "You paid in gold. You will pay in other things before the end. Let one small thing remain yours."

Polyonymous opened her mouth to ask what other things, but the lamps dimmed all at once, as if the room had drawn a breath, and Rán was gone.

Darkness followed.

Polyonymous stood in it, palms open, every part of her listening. The dark here was not empty; it felt inhabited, a velvet drape laid over a sleeping world. When the voice came, it came soft, welcoming, a woman's tone woven from patience.

"Welcome, Polyonymous."

Her name in that voice brought tears to her throat.

"I cannot see you," she said.

"You will," the voice replied. "The way I look is not quite god, human, or death. I do not wish to frighten you. I will restore the room's light at your pace."

"Who speaks."

"I am Hel," the voice said, and the name carried no threat, only a grounded calm, like earth after rain.

"Daughter of Loki. Keeper of the quiet road. Queen of what waits. You should not be afraid of me."

"I am not afraid," Polyonymous said, and was surprised to hear mostly truth in it.
Light bloomed as if dawn had been invited into the room. It revealed a hall worked with black stone polished until it held faint reflections like water.

Vines of pale metal traced the walls, and lamps burned in bowls of onyx. In the centre stood a woman robed in white that was almost silver, veil trailing like a tide. Her hair was the deep brown of old wood, and on one side her face was that of a woman alive, beautiful in a measured way, the kind of beauty that does not ask for your gaze but keeps it anyway. On the other side, the skin gave way to bone, not bloody, not ruined, but revealed, clean as carved ivory, an elegant skull exposed. A crown ringed her head, simple and un-jewelled, and in her eyes both of them there was kindness.

Polyonymous could not stop the tremble that took her knees. She sank down, tears falling before she had decided to cry. "I am dead," she whispered. "Am I dead."

Hel came forward at once and knelt with her, the hem of her robe whispering on the stone. She touched Polyonymous's hands, and they were warm.

"No," Hel said gently. "Not unless you wish to be.

If you choose it, you may remain here with me. Or you may choose to go back to your own realm, back to your body."

Polyonymous let out a breath that shook her whole frame. "I have been searching for answers," she said, eyes shut. "I do not know who I am, nor my kin, nor where I am from. Do you know. Can you help me."

Hel's thumb brushed away a tear as if kindness cost her nothing. "I know who you are," she said. "I know of your kin. I am forbidden to say. I know of your powers and your path. If you wish, you can stay with me a while. I will help you. When you choose, you can return to your body in your realm. But remember, I cannot tell you of your kin. I am bound."

Polyonymous opened her eyes. She met the gaze of the living eye and the hollow calm of the revealed bone. She expected fear. What she found was a fierce, aching relief, as if she had finally located a bearing on a starless sea. "I agree to your terms."

Hel smiled, the living half and the bared bone making a harmony that should not have been possible. She rose and offered her hand. "Then let us begin."

The days in Hel's Hall did not behave like days. Lamps burned without oil, and if there was a sun, it did not show itself. Yet Polyonymous slept and woke, and hunger came and was satisfied with food that tasted of pomegranate and dark bread and clean water pulled from a spring that sang to itself in the corner of the room. She measured time by the work they did.

Hel taught without hurry. She did not explain more than needed. She did not flatter when Polyonymous succeeded. She did not scold when Polyonymous failed. She set tasks and observed with a stillness that made Polyonymous see more sharply.

They began with sight.

"Close your eyes," Hel said. "The world is a crowded room. You do not need to shout to be heard. You need to listen differently."

Polyonymous closed her eyes. At first, she heard only the obvious: the drip of the spring, the skim of her breath. Then layers unfolded. The stone ticked softly as it cooled. Something far off moved with a low, careful tread, not animal, not human, something that respected walls. She felt the shape of her own thoughts like birds settling. When Hel spoke again, the voice came from another place entirely, not the room, but from a little above the place where fear usually perched.

"Follow the thread," Hel said. "Not with your feet. With attention."

Polyonymous reached without moving. A thread met her fingertips, thin and bright, laid from her out into the air. It led to a memory she had not chosen in years childhood rain hitting the roof of a place she could not fully see, a woman's laugh, the smell of rosemary and thunder.

Hel's hand steadied hers. "Do not tear it," she said softly. "Observe. Do not seize."

Polyonymous let breath go in a long ribbon. The thread held.

They moved next to weather.

"You are not a storm to be carried," Hel said. "You are the hand that opens the window and lets the storm pass through."

"I have needed a hammer. A sword," Polyonymous said, embarrassed by the confession, as if she had shown Hel her training wheels.

"You needed focus," Hel said. "Tools are a kind of focus. But you are older than iron."

They stood in a court open to a sky that was not a sky. It did not hold blue or clouds, but it held distance and hunger. Hel lifted her palm and the air prickled.

"Name the lightning," Hel said.

Polyonymous opened her hand. At first nothing answered. Then the hairs on her arms rose. A taste like copper and rain touched her tongue. She imagined a line, exact and thin, running from a point above her to the stone ten paces away. She did not demand. She invited.

Lightning came. It was not the wild spear that had frightened her in the caves above home. It was a clean needle of light that tapped the stone exactly where she had pictured and vanished, the air chuffing once, the stone smoking a little, a neat black star burned into it.

Polyonymous laughed, the sound startling in the quiet court. "Again," she said, greedy now. "Again," Hel allowed, with the tiniest smile.

They called thunder but not the reckless kind that shattered. They learned to place sound the way one sets a cup on a table, precisely, without spill. They learned the patience of wind, how to ask it to turn back a torch, how to borrow its hand to lift a veil of fog. When Polyonymous's temper flared, as it sometimes did, Hel did not chide. She waited until the flare passed and said, "You have heat to spare. Good. Learn to pour it into a lamp, not the curtains."
On the second not-day, Hel placed a bowl in Polyonymous's hands, a simple stone dish filled with water so clear it looked like air trying to remember itself.

"Look," Hel said.

Polyonymous looked and saw only herself at first, but the reflection did not sit still. It rippled and became the forest above the cliff near the sea, her dragon's little footprints like commas in the mud.

Then Ragnar's hand, rough, brushing hair away from her temple. Then a long hall where men argued over maps while a bear slept discreetly under a table like an oversize rug.

The images kept arriving, right up until the bowl trembled in her hands.

"Enough," Hel said, covering the bowl with her palm. "Scrying is like smelling spices. You do not open every jar at once."

Polyonymous nodded, dizzy but elated. "I could feel where the next picture wanted to be."

"Good," Hel said. "You are beginning to listen to the tilt of the weave."

On the third not-day, Hel guided her to a high balcony that looked over the quiet roads of the realm. Souls moved there like travellers in a city at night, some quick, some halting, some pausing as if to listen to their own footsteps. Polyonymous felt a tenderness for them so sudden and fierce it bent her.

"Compassion is not a weakness," Hel said, beside her. "Here, it is law. Power without compassion is a poorly sharpened blade. It cuts what you did not mean to cut."

Polyonymous stood with her hands pressed to the cool stone. "I feel close to you," she said, surprised by the rawness in her voice. "As if I have known you longer than three days that are not days."

Hel considered her, that living gaze and that calm bone making a single, steady attention. "Closeness is not counted in suns," she said. "It is counted in truth. We have not lied to each other."

"Then let me say another truth. I am grateful." Hel inclined her head. "Then take another piece of truth with you. Your training is complete for now. If you choose it, you may go back. If you wish, you may stay with me."

Polyonymous turned from the view. "If I stay, I think I will forget why I left. If I return, I will miss you."

"Both can be true," Hel said. "Choose anyway."
Polyonymous drew a breath, steady and full. "I will go back."

"Then go," Hel said. "And remember. If you ever need me, use the sight we have strengthened together. Call, and I will come. Also, though I am forbidden to name your kin, there is someone who can when you return. Go to the sea witch. She was married to my father, Loki, for a time. She will know, and she will not care about the consequences of what comes out of her mouth."

Polyonymous made a face despite herself. "That sounds like a delight and a disaster."

"Yes," Hel said, a thread of humor in her tone. "Often both."

Polyonymous stepped forward and, without protocol or prayer, embraced Hel. The queen of the quiet roads returned the hug without stiffness, and for a heartbeat Polyonymous felt anchored the way a ship feels the seabed through its chain.

"Thank you," Polyonymous whispered.
"Go well," Hel said. "Go awake."

Polyonymous did not remember closing her eyes. She only knew that when she opened them, breath punched back into a chest that hurt with the suddenness of it. The ceiling above her was the familiar wood of her own chamber. The lamp leaned where it always leaned. The window held the pale idea of dawn. Dreki snored from the hearth like a kettle. Ragnar's cloak lay folded on the chair, as if waiting for a shoulder.
She touched her palms together. They tingled as if they remembered lightning.

"Awake," she said to the room, to herself, to
the road she had walked, and to the one
waiting.

"Awake."

From somewhere far, far below the world, as if
from the other side of a long, still river, a voice
that could have been a thought answered,
warm and certain.

Always.

Chapter 28 – Two Kings, One Queen, and a Journey Beyond

Polyonymous stirred. Her eyelids fluttered against the golden light spilling through the window, her body aching as though she had wrestled with gods in her sleep. The first sound she heard was a deep, joyful growl followed by a high-pitched squeal.

"Þorri, stop pushing!" Dreki's tail knocked a table over as he bounded forward, nearly trampling poor Máni, who zipped around his legs in a frenzy of excitement. The dragons' joyful chaos filled the chamber, their wings flapping, claws clattering against stone.

Polyonymous groaned but smiled, her voice

hoarse yet tinged with humour. "If I am dead, then Valhalla is far louder than I expected."

At once, the doors burst open. Ragnar stormed in, his hair wild, his chest plate hastily thrown on, eyes full of fire. Halsten followed close behind, his stride slower but no less determined, the coolness in his gaze betraying the heat of his worry.

"Polyonymous," Ragnar breathed, rushing to her side. "You rise!"

Halsten was there a heartbeat later, kneeling by her bed, taking her hand with a gentleness that almost silenced the dragons. "You're awake, my queen. Finally."

She looked at them both, her lips twitching into a shaky laugh. "I know I'm not dead… but am I dreaming or awake? In front of me stand my two kings, my two hearts, both in the same castle. Tell me, did Hel play one last trick on me?"

Ragnar and Halsten shot each other a glare sharp enough to cut steel.

"She is my wife," Ragnar growled.

"She is my queen," Halsten snapped.

Polyonymous chuckled, though it hurt her ribs. "Rest easy, both of you. I am too tired to referee your wrestling match over my affections."

The men stood, both reluctant to leave her side. "Rest," they said in unison, before glaring at each other again. With a muttered curse about Odin's balls, Ragnar stormed out first. Halsten lingered a moment, brushing his lips against her hand, before following. The dragons remained, curling protectively at her feet.

The next morning, sunlight spilled across the chamber once again. Polyonymous sat upright, her strength returning, though her heart weighed heavy. Ragnar stood at her side, Dreki's snout pressed against his leg. Halsten stood opposite, Þorri looming behind him like a silent shadow.

"My loves," she said softly, "I must tell you of what I saw. Hel took me, and she helped me. She showed me pieces of myself I never knew. But my journey… my journey is not yet done."

Ragnar's jaw clenched. "Then tell me where, and I will march beside you."

Halsten added firmly, "Or I."

She shook her head, smiling sadly. "No. Ragnar, you must return to your castle, with Dreki and Máni. Halsten, you and Þorri must stay here, in your keep. Each of you rules, each of you carries responsibility. My path is mine alone, until I know who and what I am meant to be."

Their faces fell, sorrow etched in every line. She rose slowly, pain flashing in her limbs, but she stepped forward and embraced them both. "I love you. But I cannot have a king-husband in every realm, no matter how much my dreams wish it so." She laughed nervously, her humour masking her breaking heart.

Ragnar held her tight for a long moment before stepping back, his eyes wet but fierce. "By Odin's balls, woman, you tear me apart. But I will wait. I will wait until the gods themselves tell me to stop."

Halsten pressed his forehead against hers. "You are my queen. No distance will change that."

That evening, Ragnar returned to his castle with Dreki and Máni at his heels. The halls that once rang with laughter were silent, the hearth dimmer without Polyonymous' light. Ragnar sank into his chair by the fire, the dragons sprawling beside him. Dreki slobbered across his face in a clumsy attempt at comfort. Ragnar growled, half laughing, half weeping.

"Odin's hairy balls, you beasts. She will return. She must."

Meanwhile, Polyonymous descended the
mountains alone. The wind whipped her hair,
the valleys stretched vast and endless before
her, and yet her resolve carried her step by
step. Days later, she reached the port, the smell
of salt and tar filling her lungs.

The tavern by the docks was dim and noisy,
sailors brawling in corners, tankards spilling
ale across the floor. She pushed inside, hood
drawn low. Her eyes fell upon the notice
board, where parchment fluttered in the
breeze.

She froze.

WANTED , Aurelya & Medusa.
If seen, contact Loki, Andreus, or Thor.
Details of residence enclosed.

Polyonymous burst into laughter, covering her

mouth as tears of mirth stung her eyes. "Wanted posters? As if they were mere pickpockets!" She shook her head. "The village gossip has grown ambitious."

The barkeep eyed her, frowning. "What's so funny, lass?"

She turned, smiling brilliantly. "Do you know anyone with a ship and crew for rent? I'll pay twenty gold."

He leaned against the counter, sipping from his mug. "Aye, I've got a ship. But twenty gold won't get you far. Forty's the price if you're sailing where I think you are."

"Thirty," Polyonymous countered smoothly.

He grinned, extending his hand. "Sold. Where to, then?"

She clasped it, her eyes alight with determination. "To the sea witch."

The tavern fell silent for a breath as the words hung in the air. Then, with a clap of his hands, the barkeep laughed. "By Odin's balls, woman, you've got fire in you. Very well. At dawn, we sail."

Final Chapter – The Sea Witch's Whisper

The storm clawed at the cliffs, waves howling like wolves. Salt stung Polyonymous' lips as the spray lashed her skin, her hair wild in the wind. She stood at the very edge of the jagged black rocks, her boots slick with seawater, watching the sea boil.

From the abyss rose Angrboða.

Her eyes glowed green as serpent-fire, her hair twisting with weeds and kelp, dripping trails of black water that hissed as they struck the stone. When she spoke, her voice did not echo it crawled, seeping straight into Polyonymous' bones.

"You seek answers, little queen." The witch's

grin was wide and cruel, white as broken shells. "But answers are a burden heavier than any crown."

Polyonymous steadied her breath, forcing her voice past the pounding in her chest. "Tell me why I dream. Why I love men I've never met. Why I wake only to lose them. Why every kiss feels eternal, and every death feels final."

Angrboða's laughter rolled like thunder under the sea. "Dream?" She tilted her head, water dripping from her chin. "You do not dream, child. You walk. By night you lie with kings, by day you slay them. You are the bridge between realms the wound, and the weapon."

The sea hissed and bowed to her shadow as she stepped forward.

"Do you not know who you are, girl?" she

hissed. "You are Brynhildr's daughter, steel-born Valkyrie. But your father… your father is thunder. You are Thor's blood. And through him, Odin's seed burns in you still."

Polyonymous staggered back, the spray mixing with the sudden tears she didn't want to admit had risen.

The witch's voice swelled with the storm. "Thor's passion, Odin's fate. Together, they make you more than mortal, more than Valkyrie. It makes you kin to my children Fenrir, Jörmungandr, Hel. They are your cousins, little dream-walker."

The waves rose higher, towering walls of black water crowned with lightning.

"You are a threat to their throne," Angrboða spat, foam flying from her lips. "Because if the gods should fall, if the old order breaks, you not they will be the one the realms look to. The thunder-daughter. The Valkyrie's heir. The granddaughter of fate itself."

Behind her, the sea writhed. Two figures rose from the boiling surf Aurelya, her golden hair tangled with pearls and salt, her eyes wide with warning; and Medusa, serpents hissing, eyes blazing with power. They stood half-shrouded in seafoam, as if caught between drowning and living.

Angrboða caressed them with claws of obsidian.
"My mermaids," she crooned. "My servants. And soon, you will join them… or drown beneath them."

Lightning split the sky. Polyonymous' heart thudded like war drums. She drew her blade, the storm casting firelight against the steel.

"Try me, sea-witch," she whispered.

By dawn, she was back on dry land. Captain Belladonna's Vex had cut through the storm to return her to the village. Polyonymous disembarked in silence, her boots crunching over wet gravel as she strode toward the tavern.

Inside, sailors muttered about omens, but she ignored them. She crossed to the notice board, where the ridiculous parchment fluttered once more:

WANTED Aurelya & Medusa.
If seen, contact Loki, Andreus, or Thor.
Details of residence enclosed.

With a wry grin, she tore it down, rolled it in her fist, and demanded directions from the locals.

By dusk, she stood at a carved wooden door, her knuckles poised. She knocked.

It creaked open, and a cluster of small sea-witch children spilled out, squealing, tugging at her cloak, and darting between her legs. They dragged her inside with giggles, their webbed fingers leaving little trails of saltwater on the floor.

"Don't stand out there," a voice called. "Come in."

Polyonymous lifted her chin, stepping into the candlelit hall. At the long table sat three men: Andreus, dark and calculating; Loki, smirking with sly amusement; and Thor, broad-shouldered, thunder still clinging to his presence like perfume.

Polyonymous' gaze locked on Thor's.

She stepped forward, her voice steady though her heart pounded with fire and grief.

"Hello, Father."

About the Author

Holly Symons is a storyteller who walks the thin line between dreams and waking life. With a lifelong passion for mythology, fantasy, and epic adventure, she weaves tales that blur the boundaries of what is real and what is imagined.

In *I Am Polyonymous: And Every Night I Live Dream Walking*, Holly brings to life a heroine who moves between realms, carrying the weight of love, loss, and destiny in every step. Her writing blends cinematic intensity with moments of humour, heart, and raw humanity echoing her own journey of navigating life with imagination as both compass and refuge.

This book forms part of a much larger saga, *The Realmsverse of Mirrors*, an

interconnected series where gods, dream-
walkers, and myth-touched mortals collide
across realms. Each story stands on its own, yet
together they weave a tapestry of epic battles,
heartbreak, and the enduring power of love
and choice.

When Holly isn't dream-walking through her
stories, she can be found surrounded by
dragons (the fictional kind), laughter, and an
ever-growing library of books that fuel her
next adventures. Her mission is simple: to
remind readers that no dream is too wild, no
love too impossible, and no story too strange to
be told.